THIS MAN DID I KILL?

"Help me!" Janetta screamed, in her nightmare, but no one came.

Janetta is convulsed with guilt, tormented with nameless fears. Her first husband is mysteriously dead, her second a crude, passionate, thoughtless bully, demanding and jealous . . .

Like an animal in a trap she twists and turns, tearing at herself — *Did I kill my first husband? Can I have done such a thing and have forgotten it?*

"Help me!" she cries — and at last there is hope, for Dr. Emmanuel Cellini hears, and his unorthodox comprehension of the human heart and mind will unearth the truth, free the innocent, end the nightmares . . .

THIS MAN DID I KILL? —

The 10th story of Dr. Emmanuel Cellini

by

JOHN CREASEY

as

MICHAEL HALLIDAY

HODDER AND STOUGHTON
LONDON SYDNEY AUCKLAND TORONTO

C49128

Contents

BOOK I

Through the eyes of
JANETTA

1

The Longing

I DID NOT DARE TO OPEN MY EYES. I KNEW WHAT I WOULD see, so close above me. I knew, from all that had gone before, from what was happening now, from the pressure and the thrust of this man whom I had married, what he would be like.

The foreshortened view of his unshaven face. The dark stubble, rough, scratching wherever it touched my cheek, my forehead, my nose, even my lips. The rounded chin, the lower lip drawn back so that I could see the small, uneven teeth in his lower jaw. The tautness; in every muscle of his face as well as of his body.

The ugliness. The beast in him. Who but a beast would force himself upon his mate, no matter how she felt?

I did not dare to open my eyes: and yet I opened them. It was as if some awful compulsion made me; as if I no longer had command of my eyes, as if I had lost control of them as well as of the rest of my limp, brutalised body.

I saw what I had known I would see: his teeth clenched, his eyes staring open, his nostrils distended, the breath forcing itself through them as if his throat were tightly closed; constricted.

He began to gasp . . .

I was in the grip of a whirlwind; every part of me; and instead of life pouring into me, I felt as if all life were gushing out. This was how it had always been, ever since the early days of our marriage. I could not go on, it had to end.

I thought: *If only I could kill him.* If only I could kill him, if only I could kill, could kill, could kill ...

That was the birth of the horror which came to possess me. It was like a revelation: like conception. It touched me first with an icy coldness, then set me shivering.

I was aware of the shivering, that my teeth were chattering, that my eyes were closed now as if great clamps were holding down the lids. There was worse. There were flashes in my head and across my eyes. Vivid, yellow, livid flashes; as if lightning had drowned the pale light of the landing. Awful, agonising flashes, like knife thrusts; agonising.

There was a noise as of thunder.

I knew that he was shouting at me: bellowing close to my ear.

I felt his hands on my shoulders; strong hands which could be so brutal and yet so gentle. I felt the pain of his fingers biting into the flesh of my shoulders and yet compared with the pain at my eyes as the lightning flashed, that was not hurt at all. He was roaring; *bellowing.*

"Open your eyes!" he yelled. "Open them! Janetta, open them! Every time you spoil things for me ... Open your *eyes*!"

He began to shake me so that my head rose up and then fell back on the mattress, the firm mattress, hard, which he preferred. Early in his paroxysm the pillows had been thrown aside.

"Open your eyes Janetta, open your eyes!"

He was rearing up, away from me; astride yet hardly touching, except where he gripped my shoulders and shook me up and down, up and down, my head banging, my teeth snapping, the lightning still flashing in my eyes and the pain spreading.

Suddenly, he stopped. All I could hear was his heavy breathing. He, who so loved to rest, relax, lie still, gasping for breath. Now, it was I who lay still, conscious only of the flashes and the pain in my head; oblivious of my nakedness, oblivious of his.

Still.

His breathing quietened, and through the noises which now filled my ears, he spoke again: just one word — my name.

"Janetta."

I was aware of the word, even of the strange way in which he uttered it, but other words were passing through my mind, as if with returning consciousness I relived what I had been thinking and saying. If only I could kill him, could kill, could kill, could kill . . .

"Janetta!" Now his voice was hoarse and edged with fear. "Janetta — open your eyes."

They were closed so tightly that it seemed as if they were sealed forever.

Still hoarsely, he whispered: "Janetta! You can't be — "

I felt his hand beneath my breast; finding its way gently now, not in the brutal force of the beginning.

"Janetta — "

And he was feeling for my pulse. That was when I realised that he thought, or at least feared, that I was dead; and that was when I understood his horror. But for my own, I might have found it a macabre joke; that he should fear that he had done to me what I had longed to do to him.

I even wondered in those few seconds if I were dead; if death brought no release but even greater awareness of pain and anguish, distress and dismay, but suddenly he spoke again in a different, rougher voice:

"You're not dead. Come on, shake out of it." And after a moment he went on: "Open your eyes."

I tried to, then. There would be no horrid sight close to me; for he had moved and was at the side of the bed, his fingers still at my wrist but the other hand no longer beneath my breast. I would have looked at him then because I knew that once my eyes opened he would be calmer, that if I kept them closed his anger would rise and he would rage because he would think I was defying him.

I tried to say: "I can't."

A kind of paralysis gripped me; and I was still cold.

I heard him move further from the bed, and felt a breath of wind — and then a sharp blow on the side of my face, delivered with his open hand. My head jolted to one side, perhaps my eyelids fluttered; but I could not see him, because my eyes did not open. I knew he was standing and glaring down at me, for I could hear his heavy breathing some way off.

Would he strike again? I wondered but had no sense of fear, not even of apprehension: it was as if my muscles, my nerves, were keeping my eyes tightly closed so that I could not see the horror which had been born in me. I do not know how long we were like that but there was time at least for his breathing to steady, for his rage to fade. When he spoke again it was in a husky voice; touched, perhaps, with pleading.

"Do you really hate me so?"

I tried to speak, but could not; no muscle moved, at my eyes or mouth or body, yet my mind was alert; as if it were held in the calm before a nightmare. He began to move about the room, and I could imagine his picking up his clothes and mine; suddenly, I was aware that he was nearer; I could feel the softness of his breath on my cheek. I thought, he is going to kiss me, and had no feeling of revulsion, still less of pleasure; my body was like a statue made of ice.

He did not kiss me. With an exclamation he moved away, and next moment I felt a sheet being drawn up over me, then a blanket, unfolded; and another. He left them loose, and I sensed that he stood looking down at me before he turned and went out of the room. He did not close the door.

I heard him moving about, first in the bathroom, making the little hard sounds of glass and toothbrush on the porcelain; the click of the closing of the cabinet door; the running of water and the subdued roar of the flush. As he came on to the landing and crossed to the spare room the floorboards creaked; soon, bed springs creaked; he had left that room door open, too.

All this time, I neither moved nor opened my eyes. The utter stillness was both familiar and strange; familiar in that I knew I had known, or experienced, it before, strange because it was so different from anything in ordinary life. It was not the stillness which followed sleep, or the stillness of the suspension of mind and body before sleep. It was more as if I had been struck down; had it come upon me when I had been standing, I would have fallen; and I believed I would have lain where I had fallen, as unmoving as I was now.

These were less thoughts than reflections; awareness; as if I were both inside and outside myself, standing as Marcus had stood by the side of the bed, looking down at me as I lay on my back. I was aware that my legs and my body had straightened; my legs were touching at the inner thighs, knees and ankles.

There was a change; the lightning flashes were farther away. They had not ceased altogether but they no longer slashed across my eyes and through my head, and although my head ached it was not with the crackling pain I had known when and immediately after I had opened my eyes and looked at him; when I had thought, if only I could kill him. If only I could kill.

I shivered as the phrase lit itself up in my mind: *If only I could kill him.*

Could kill, could kill, could kill...

I began to sweat and to shiver; I was hot one moment and icy cold the next. The shivering worsened, was an ague which possessed my whole body. Thighs, knees, ankles touched, bone tapping against bone. It was not only my body but my arms and legs, every muscle twitched, my teeth began to chatter, my whole being went out of control with a shivering and a shaking far worse than I had ever known. It was as if Marcus had flung himself on me again with a violence greater, far greater than he had ever shown even in his wildest paroxysms: but he was not there, no great weight was on me. I was alone and my body jumped, my head shook, everything inside me seemed to become loose: loose at first and then like jelly.

It would not stop.

It was utterly uncontrollable, so full of fury that my whole body was lifted from the bed, and dropped, tremors began somewhere inside me and spread out to all my extremities, making my legs kick and my arms shake as if they would free themselves from their sockets; it was convulsion so absolute that a new terror came upon me: that it would never stop, that nothing I could do would bring back that strange and precious stillness.

I had shaken like this before; often. *I could not go on living in such a way.*

Out of the awareness of the present convulsions there was recollection of being tossed about helplessly before, of being hurled great distances and yet all the time left there.

I could imagine great hands, holding, rolling, pushing, thrusting, lifting, dropping, shaking me; and then in awful convulsive movements doing all these things at once so that my head felt as if it were being shaken from my neck, and my hands from my wrists and my feet from my ankles. As if all my bones had broken or else turned to jelly so that they could not resist the all-conquering power of the force that tormented me.

On, on, it went, never stopping. I knew that my mouth opened and closed, that I bit at the pillow as at last I turned, writhing, that my fingers began to clutch at the side of the bed, at the pillow. I was frozen in hideous coldness. I was burning as if in a great fire. I was gasping, groaning, crying out: "Help me, help me, help me."

Nothing and no one helped me, I was at the mercy of this force.

"Help me!" I screamed in nightmare. "Help me!"

No one came. There was near darkness, that was all — darkness and solitariness. I was utterly alone; no one would, no one could help me. I knew this now as I had known it in the past; when I had been the victim of these convulsions, gripped by this nightmare which was not a dream but real. I was not convulsed because of sleep, I was conscious of every shake, every movement, every pain, every moment of the torture; conscious and alone.

I had always been alone when these had seized me. Alone . . .

I was always alone, and was afraid of solitude. Terrified. I had known only loneliness all my life, wherever I had been, with whomever I had been, and now I was helpless and my body was battered and I cried out in the dread convulsions the cry which I recognised, remembering it from my earliest days.

"Help me, help me, help me."

"Help me!"

But no one ever came.

No one had come in those childhood days, the beginning of loneliness, the first awareness of its pain and anguish; no one had ever come, until the peak of the need had been reached and climbed, leaving me limp and still and silent.

My body was in torment. *"Help me!"* My body was on fire. *"Help me!"* My body was frozen with a searing cold. Help — help — help me!

Help me!

I tried to fling the sheet and the blanket off but could not grip them, I tried to move from the bed but those unseen hands held and shook and tossed and beat me, I did not think I could live during the thrashing and the threshing.

Help me!

Suddenly, there were sounds beyond this room, and footsteps; there was a click and light came on, there was Marcus, a huge figure in pale blue, crying my name: "Janetta, Janetta!" My back was towards him, the convulsions reached a screaming intensity, worse, far worse than they had been before.

He was on the other side of the bed, bending over me.

"Janetta! Oh, my God, Janetta!"

There was wildness in his eyes, the wildness of alarm, of fear, not anger, and now he muttered under his breath: "Oh, my God." He turned away, I was just aware of him moving, then aware that he was piling blankets over me. A drawer squeaked open, he pulled out an eiderdown, stored there for the summer, and draped it over me. I tried to speak but could not, my teeth were cracking against one another, I bit my tongue and caused new, sharper pain.

. .

He was sobbing.

"Janetta, what is it? Janetta!" And then he cried: "Don't worry, I'll never do that again. I swear I won't!"

He would never stop.

Why didn't he help me now — ?

As that question came into my mind I knew that he was helping; as far as he ever could, he was helping, and although I was so awfully alone I was not utterly so, not wholly deserted.

He was helping me. This man whom I had so longed to kill, *was* helping me. This husband, this second husband I had known, was helping. And my convulsions slowly became less terrifying. As he knelt by the side of the bed, arms stretched out, I had a moment of stillness. The convulsions were dying. As they always died.

2

Suggestions

NOW AND AGAIN I SHIVERED, BUT THIS NO LONGER HURT me. The fear of shivery fits had gone; fear and pain and the sense of helplessness and hopelessness. I do not know how long I had been there, lying quieter; nor how long Marcus had stayed there, moving only a little, to ease his legs. Much of the time my eyes were closed, but whenever I opened them he was there; smiling, or trying to smile.

I no longer yearned to kill him. Not then.

It was a different face, now, the one on a level with mine. He was handsome in his dark and sombre way, with clear-cut lips and dark eyes and sharply defined eyebrows and lashes, and dark hair which swept back in waves from his forehead. Even the fact that he had not shaved no longer troubled me. This was no brute, demanding, taking, savaging: this was a gentle and yet a frightened man.

I must speak to him; must thank him. My mouth was parched, and my throat painful. My body ached but it was the ache of restfulness and relaxation, the pleasurable aching which meant that the need for effort, the bunching of muscles and the screaming of nerves were gone.

I tried to speak, but hardly opened my lips, but a light sprang to his eyes and he asked eagerly:

"Thirsty?"

I nodded, gratefully.

"I'll get you some tea," he said, and began to get up; it was an effort even for such a strong man who was so physically fit. Then he stopped, crouching, looking scared. "Will you — will you be all right?"

I nodded.

"I won't be two shakes of a lamb's tail," he promised.

I managed to smile, and that pleased him. He stood to his full height, nearly six feet, towering over me, and smiling again. The perspective was different, suddenly I was reminded of the way he had looked when all I could think of was killing him. I shivered and closed my eyes, but either he did not notice or he decided to waste no more time, so he went out, and I lay still.

I was warm, now. That momentary flashback to terror faded, and did not disturb me again. I lay on my left side, facing the wall of this, our house, the little suburban house, so secret, so private, one among hundreds yet so isolated; but I did not dwell on those things now.

Opposite me was a small dressing-table, with a few oddments on it: brushes, a comb; a hand-mirror, backed in *petit point*. A glass tray and a ring stand with my two rings held also a lipstick, some small bottles of make-up, all I needed. And there was a tiny bottle of perfume, Chanel; at once a joy for the pleasure it gave and an anxiety because there was so little left.

On the chair by the side of the bed were my clothes; bra, slip, tights. So fragile-looking.

Above the dressing-table was a mirror and in this I could see the doorway, and the dim light on the landing, the bright light from the tiny bathroom. In the bathroom was an electric kettle, and everything needed for making tea and coffee: and there was milk, too, and sugar. Even in the small house it sometimes seemed a long way to the kitchen which was immediately beneath this room.

He was in the kitchen; I could hear him.

I lay with the newfound comfort and the warmth, the 'nightmare' past, not listening, not thinking, and knowing why I did not let myself think. If I did, I would be touched again if not possessed by fear.

Now and again a tiny spasm caught me and contracted my heart, but it did not last.

I began to doze, and yet was glad when I heard Marcus on the stairs, and I turned to face the doorway. I smiled at him, and his answering smile had never been broader or more relaxed: I realised how frightened he had been. He came in and put the tray on a corner of the dressing-table, pushing the tray to one side, and I began to sit up. I had forgotten my nakedness. He had forgotten, too. For a moment each of us went still; an awful moment which carried us back in time.

Then, I said: "Will you put the eiderdown round my shoulders?"

"Of course!" He picked it up and draped it over me, folding it at the breast so that it would not gape. I saw tension on his face but it did not last for long. "Comfortable?"

"Lovely," I said.

"You look — " he began, but broke off.

"How do I look?" I asked.

It was not that I really wanted him to tell me; only, that I wanted him to feel that he could, that he could truly relax. And he did relax, and actually laughed.

"Beautiful," he said.

"Impossible," I retorted.

"Do you remember that saying about beauty being in the eye of the beholder?"

"Vaguely," I replied. It was one of his favourite

phrases. I moistened my dry lips and countered with another banality: "Why did you have to go downstairs?"

"I thought you might prefer something cold, and there wasn't enough milk up here."

I *had* to humour him; help him; try at least to soothe the hurt I had inflicted.

"A little cold milk," I said, "and a lot of piping hot tea!"

"That's the ticket! I could go to Ovaltine, too."

"You have the Ovaltine," I said. I detested all milk drinks — except cold milk itself.

He gave me half a cupful of milk, fresh from the refrigerator; cold and sharp and exactly what I needed; then poured out tea as I like it, weak, without sugar and with only a little milk. He poured himself tea from another pot: he liked his very strong and with a lot of sugar. He moved to the corner of the bed, our double bed, one leg under him, the other stretched out alongside mine; he could be comfortable for long periods in poses which would soon make me stiff.

We drank . . .

"Good?" he asked.

"Just right."

"Feel — feel better?"

"Much," I assured him.

He moistened his lips, and looked like a small boy; he could behave so boyishly at times and it was hard to believe that he was in the late thirties: in fact, thirty-eight, ten years older than I. From where I sat he looked handsome and virile and — wholesome. Yes, wholesome. *'Each man in his time plays many parts.'* Each man, in his life, is not one but a dozen men, each different, each whole.

"Janetta," he said, "do you want to talk?"

The inescapable fact was that he and I would never

really be able to talk, not in the true sense — my sense. Another was that I abhorred the thought of talking at these times. Yet if we did not, there would be tomorrow, hanging over our heads, over my head, like a shadow. I thought, inanely, to talk or not to talk, that is the question; and *I* accused Marcus of banality!

If we discussed what had happened now, then perhaps — perhaps — for a few days there would be no need for discussion, there might even be a longer period of contentment: or at least, freedom from disquiet and the apprehension I had come to live with and which I so hated.

If we discussed it now, then Marcus might find it easier to sleep; to go to his office in the morning; to live normally.

His eyes were pleading; those great brown eyes which could hold the sadness of a spaniel — and the fire of a lion.

So I said: "If you would like to, Marcus, of course."

Yet talking to him now was the last thing I wanted; a mood of distaste — no, stronger, revulsion — swept over me and I had to clench my teeth not to show the swift change in my mood. He looked over my head as he often did when thinking embarrassing things, and that gave me a moment's respite; but it did not hold back the tremor which ran through my body.

When he looked straight at me again, I was calm enough outwardly but inwardly agitated.

"Janetta," he said, "I love you more than I can possibly tell you."

Love? Need? Desire? *Love?*

"I know," I lied. "I know."

"And I know you don't feel the same way towards me."

This was following a pattern so familiar that I could almost hear his sentences three, four, five or six ahead.

The predictability of what he would say and do sometimes drove me to distraction; I would hate even the good
thoughts, the good and kind deeds. At least I did not lie
to myself about my feelings for him, and seldom lied to
him, then only out of imagined kindness. I could damn
him and damn myself with good intentions.

"I feel differently," I said, huskily. "Differently."

"Janetta," he said, and paused; there were times when
he began every sentence with my name, as if it were an
invocation to a goddess or a priestess. "Why *did* you
marry me?"

Oh, dear God: *that* question.

I did not answer.

"Surely — surely you must have loved me, then."

Love? I had been so desperately lonely, so frightened,
so helpless on my own. I had needed protection, the
warmth of friendship and companionship, someone to
talk to; to go places with: a companion not a lover, a
friend and not a husband. But I had told him none of
these things, I had lied to him. I lied again now.

"Yes," I said. "Of course I did."

"Janetta," he said, leaning forward, but still so far
away that he could not really touch me; not with intimacy
or the hope of intimacy, "do you think it would help if —
if we had separate bedrooms? If — if I kept away from
you for a few weeks, even a few months?"

I caught my breath, I was so surprised.

"Do you?" The appeal in his voice held a throb, it
was so intense. "It — it would be damned hard, but — if
you think it would help — "

Help? It would be like heaven on earth; it would be
freedom from dread of the man he became when passion
stirred him; it would be freedom from the reminders of
awful fears, the brightening of shadows so dark they
could turn night into day. Help? It could let me breathe,

and live, and even laugh, but — how could I tell him so?

When, in the past, I had even hinted that we might stop sharing a bed, he had been savage with fury; raged; hurled insults at me, deep reproach, bitter, hurtful things. That all I wanted was a free home, free food, the comforts of a home without any of the obligations; and in this revelation of himself he had shown what I had known for a long, long time: his obsession with sex.

The house could go to rack and ruin, the food be ruined, too; I could look a frump, a freak, but satisfy the lust in him and nothing else at all would matter. Oh, there were times when he seemed to forget, when he genuinely tried to see and treat me as a human being, not simply as a physical mate, but —

I had hesitated so long before replying that he must know what an honest reply would be: "Yes, yes, yes!" I expected a frown to begin to gather at his forehead, the familiar groove to form between his eyes, but his expression did not change. He was very pale, but his expression simply did not change.

"Or would you rather go away?" he asked.

Go away? It was as if the world were coming to an end, and I heard what he went on to say although I was still bewildered and incredulous.

"You could go somewhere on the coast, or if you preferred it, even to the Continent for a week or so. Several weeks. I'm sure you need rest, darling. What happened tonight couldn't have happened if you weren't overwrought and over-tired."

I simply could not find words.

"Think about it," he urged, after a while. "There's no hurry, so far as I'm concerned — except that the sooner you begin the rest cure the sooner you'll be yourself again!"

He actually laughed.

I could not believe this was happening: that this was Marcus.

Now if he were Anthony —

The thought cut through me like a knife. *If he were Anthony*, for Anthony would have talked this way and looked like this, but Anthony was dead. My first husband was dead. *If Marcus were Anthony*. If wishes were horses. *If Marcus were Anthony*. God, dear God, what was happening to me, to Marcus? He was beginning to talk and even to look like Anthony. No, no, no! It was a trick of my mind. *Help me, help me, help me*. If Marcus were Anthony, if wishes were horses, how I wish I could kill him; how I wish I could kill, kill, kill . . .

"There's one other possibility," Marcus was saying. "One other thing you might like to do." He did not wait for me to ask what it was, he seemed to know that I was dumbstruck; I had not said an intelligible word since he had begun to show this new side to himself. "You might like to see a doctor," he went on. "Would you, Janetta?"

This time, I had to answer.

I had a feeling that this was what he had been leading up to; that this was the question which really mattered, and the two proposals, that we should have separate rooms or that I should go away on my own had been simply to soften my mind, to prepare me for what he really wanted to suggest.

I found myself asking: "What kind of doctor do you mean?"

"Oh, any good doctor. I think you need a tonic, somehow or other you've managed to get run down." Quite without warning, Marcus straightened out the leg he was sitting on and swung himself off the bed. "Think about all three," he urged. "And we'll talk again tomorrow." He moved towards me, bent down and kissed my forehead, then — quite unable to help himself — thrust his hand beneath the eiderdown and caressed me, not roughly and yet with a reminder of roughness.

"Goodnight," he said gruffly, and rounded the bed and went out.

This time, he closed the door.

I did not try to find the words, did not move, I simply sat with the eiderdown folded back, aware of the rough touch of his hand, and its coldness, and I found a phrase bounding back in my mind.

If only I could kill him, kill him, kill him.

If only I could kill.

3

Quiet

WHAT IS THE MATTER WITH ME? I WHISPERED IN THE darkness. Why do I keep thinking of killing?

I lay now in a different kind of stillness, a more tense kind of fear; almost as of something supernatural. I went over what had happened time and time again, forcing myself to recall every little incident, movement, sound, from the time he had come into my room so long ago.

It seemed as if it had been in another age. Why had I felt so strongly tonight? Why had I wanted to kill Marcus? Nothing had been different: not really different.

On such nights my mind seemed to close; to freeze; I felt a deep and compelling need not to know, not *know* what was happening. In its way that was a form of madness, for of course I knew, and felt the revulsion, never pleasure, never hope of pleasure, yet I was — or for four years now I had been — able to be two selves; the compliant self, the vehicle for his passion, and the self which did not really know or understand — no, which did not feel.

There were these two parts of me.

There had been, I reminded myself, for four years, so — why had tonight been a greater horror? Why had the two selves merged in that mood of revulsion so great that I hated him so and wanted him dead?

I did not know.

I remembered the sudden coldness; the lightning inside my head; a sense of terror. I remembered the sense of being possessed but not by Marcus, by some awful thing; but I did not know what that thing was, only that it filled me with such fear.

I must forget . . .

It was impossible to forget!

I must make myself think of the kindness he had shown, the gentle side of his nature, his obvious longing to help me, but although I could remember all he had said and done I felt no emotional response, no true gratitude. No one could have said or done more. I remembered my astonishment when he had first suggested that we should have separate rooms, or that I should go away on my own; or see a doctor. Even the astonishment did not fill the emotional gap I knew was there; did not make me feel the gratitude that I knew I should feel.

At least, he had left me. The door was closed and I was alone. It was quiet in the room; the small gilt travelling-clock's faint tick-tick-tick-tick was hardly audible. A long way off there were the night sounds: of cars on the main road, of aeroplanes, even farther away the rumble of a train, for we lived in a southern suburb, far out of London, in fact in Surrey, not far from the main line from Waterloo Station to Bournemouth and Southampton, to the south and the south-west; far enough away from London Airport not to find the engines even of the mammoth planes disturbing but near enough to know they were up there, waiting to land, perhaps, or surging forward with the great black trails behind them, eager to go.

These sounds were really part of the night; the silence. Nearer noises might disturb me: a car in this street, Henley Street; or the banging of a gate or the closing of a door. Each small house had its own small garden, most of them cared for; each garden had its path of crazy-paving or cement, or gravel, or even red brick, laid with loving care.

This house had crazy-paving, and an iron gate, painted white; I had painted it white. Some of the stones were loose, and made a dull thud of sound when one walked on them; and the gate squeaked. Thuds and squeaks were loud in the quiet; a gate closed, farther along the row of semi-detached houses. I knew that it was a neighbour, a post-office sorter, back late; he was always late.

I heard even the closing of the front door of his house, but after that there was silence. I lay warm and snug and alone; so glad to be alone. The secret fear, new-born that night, had died, and for a while I was unaware of it.

Another sound came into the room, not from outside but from the other room; it was Marcus, snoring. The sound became louder until I turned on my side and buried my face in the pillow, pulled the blanket and the eiderdown over my ear, but still the harsh noise came through to me. I began to say under my breath: "Stop it." Then more quickly: "*Stop it, stop it, stop it!*" But it went on and on, until in place of the cry of "Stop, stop, stop!" there came the other, awful words, clear as if they were printed on my mind.

If only I could kill him.

If only I could kill . . .

Kill, kill, kill!

I screamed beneath the bedclothes, not daring to scream enough to wake him and bring him back. I began to shiver and to shake, the aches and pains came back like the echo of my voice: *Kill him, kill him, kill him!*

Suddenly, I was still.

Suddenly, I was asleep, although I did not know until the morning that the nightmare had faded into sleep and my mind as well as body was at rest.

It was daylight when I woke; sunlit day. I lay on my

side, with the clothes pulled away from my nose and mouth and eyes but still warm and snug. I was aware of the distant, daytime sounds: people walking in the street, people talking, cars moving, bicycles moving, a doorbell ringing, a gate closing with a metallic bang.

It was late; these were not early morning sounds; and the sun shining into a corner of the room was not the early morning sun.

What time was it?

Had Marcus gone, or had he overslept?

The first moment of alarm and concern came to me and I stiffened, trying to catch any sound inside the house, but there was none. He hated getting himself off. There was little enough I did, his manner seemed to say, I could at least get up and give him his breakfast: if I wanted to come back to bed after he'd left that was my affair. But my duty was to see him safely off.

Reluctantly, I pushed back the bedclothes. It was suddenly quite chilly, especially for a day in July. Cold. I gave an involuntary shiver and pushed the bedclothes farther back, then saw the message on the chair. It was a small chair from the corner of the room, with a cane seat and cane back. Standing up so that I could not fail to see the wording, as well as the card itself, was the message:

I'm on my way! See you tonight. Please, please don't worry—Marcus.

I let myself fall back into bed, slowly, but did not pull the clothes over me; I must get up. Instead I lay there, becoming more chilled with every minute, knowing a window was open, and that the door was open, too, causing a draught and the chilliness.

How could he do more to help me?

What an awful thing, that I longed to kill him.

What an awful —

"But I don't!" I cried aloud. "I can't want to kill him. It's madness!"

Madness.

At last I got out of bed.

Memories of what had happened last night crowded into my mind but they were cold and distant and did not disturb me. I washed and dressed slowly, because there was no hurry, putting on a jumper and skirt of patterned green and gold; my hair hardly needed attention, all I had to do was push it into shape. I used no powder or lipstick — I seldom did in the morning unless I were going out; or someone was coming to see me; and a prospect of a visitor was so remote it was almost laughable.

I was in no mood to laugh or cry: or to feel. The word, the thought of madness had so sobered me that I could hardly think but did everything mechanically: making coffee, toast, spreading butter and a bitter-sweet marmalade, washing up — Marcus had left an empty cereal bowl and a cup and saucer in the small stainless steel sink. The kitchen overlooked the small garden and the wooden fences which divided our tiny plot from the houses on either side and at the end of the garden itself. Each house was the same in design, built of pale red brick, with long but narrow windows. In defiance of this imposed symmetry everyone painted the woodwork in a different colour; black, white, green, blue, two houses along a vivid pink, farther along an unbelievable heliotrope. And although each garden was identical in shape and size, each was cultivated and planted differently; seen from the roof it was a patchwork of vari-shaped lawns, flower beds, vegetable rows, fruit trees. Every roof was the same colour: grey.

I dusted, polished, vacuumed each small room and

narrow passage; moved each piece of lightweight contemporary furniture, frail-looking, strong and sturdy in performance. When I had finished it was half-past twelve, and the rest of the day stretched out before me, drearily.

I could go to the public library in Hendleton, a walk and a bus ride away. I could tend the garden which was in perfect order. I could read here, the old classics I had once loved but of which I had long since wearied. Or I could go shopping.

I would walk.

Would you like to talk?

Walk, talk, walk, talk: help me, help me, help me; kill, kill, kill!

I could *see* his face above me.

"Oh, dear God, *no!*" I screamed. "Stop it, stop it!"

I must go out, staying in was affecting me, turning my mind to madness. *I must walk.* I ran upstairs and pulled open a drawer in the dressing-table, snatched up a pair of gloves, put on a pair of brown walking shoes, and ran downstairs again. It was as if the walls of the house were shouting at me.

Talk, talk, talk.

Help me, help me, help me.

Kill him, kill him, kill him!

"No," I gasped. "No, no!" I ran to the front door and turned the knob, and pulled the door open.

I saw a woman near the gate; a young woman with bright red hair.

I slammed the door and ran — *ran* — away from the screaming house and the dread monotony of the days and the hideous company of the nights. I opened the gate and heard it slam. I turned right, away from the woman with red hair, and now I began to adjure myself.

"Don't run; people will see you. Don't run, don't run."

I slowed down but continued to walk fast, aware that

I was breathing very hard, aware also that the air was fresh and cool and I no longer felt stifled, with walls closing in on me.

People passed me, but none spoke.

Young women, mostly with babies in prams or push-chairs, were walking briskly and with purpose. One old man with very white hair and a pink face looked at me curiously but I gave him no chance to speak, just hurried past. At the end of the street was a small park, more a patch of wooded land, with grass and laurel bushes, ferns and bramble, some small beech and some tall birch, the trunks silvered. The sunlight filtered through the leaves, making patterns on the path, the grass and me. On one side was a children's playground, deserted as usual in the morning, and beyond the park, half-a-mile away, was a hill with steps cut into it leading to another, much better residential area than this — which was known as Dingle Park.

On the painted wooden benches people sat, mostly old, the men reading newspapers, or talking; one old woman in a wheelchair was complaining in a high-pitched voice to a thin, woeful-looking young woman. The air was alive with birds and with insects; ever-moving.

Suddenly, I realised that I had left my bag at home.

Of all the crazy things to do —

Crazy!

Of all the idiotic things to do: run upstairs for shoes and gloves and forget my bag with purse and money, even my keys. What a fool! I went on, walking now uphill, towards the steps, although I knew I would have to go back soon. How could I shop, or even pay my bus fare? The hill slowed me down, and I was almost at a standstill when I turned and looked — not expecting what I saw — over the mass of grey roofs and the streets and the patch-work gardens.

3—TMDIK * *

The houses there were in a valley, bordered on one side by the railway embankment, on the other by an industrial area, thirty, or more factories, some small, none really large, where many of the people who lived in Dingle Park Estate worked; it was within easy cycling and reasonable walking distance. Beyond the industrial area was a main road and I could see two red buses, tiny from here, on one of the roads which led to the factories.

I had never seen this so clearly before, and wondered why. *Was* I beginning to see things which I had never noticed before? To understand things within myself as well as to see such things as this?

I realised that there had been a change. A row of tall elms had once cut off the industrial area, but the trees had been felled, revealing the extra ugliness.

I grimaced: what a place to live.

I thought back to my childhood, and the country, and to laughter and family, to company, to a time before this loneliness had come so acutely upon me.

Tears stung my eyes.

"Idiot!" I exclaimed aloud. "Take hold of yourself!"

Yet as I walked down the hill I fought a battle with myself: I did not want to go back, I had run away to brief freedom, and I felt that going back was going to prison.

Madness!

Marcus had offered to let me go away, hadn't he?

Not for always, just for a few weeks, but weeks, even days, could help enormously, could help me to find myself, would keep me away from danger.

From what danger?

A voice inside my head began to scream: Kill him, kill him, kill him!

4

The New Neighbour

THE HOUSE WAS ONLY FIFTY YARDS OR SO AWAY.

The black and white of the woodwork and the ironwork stood out against pastel colours on either side. The single flowering cherry tree in the middle of the square lawn was unmistakable, too, its foliage so thick and casting shadow over the front room downstairs.

Two or three gates along was a removal van, the back open, two men inside; they were shifting a piano on to a trolley, something I could not fail to notice for I so wanted a piano. The van appeared to be nearly empty of furniture. I turned into my gate, and closed it quietly this time, reached the front door and then remembered that I had no key.

It was not a disaster. It had happened before, and I knew exactly what to do, but stood without moving, in futile panic. I clenched my hands and gritted my teeth; could have screamed, or turned and ran.

I did not want to go into the house again.

All would have been well, or at least tolerable, had I been able to open the door and step inside without pause, without hindrance: but now the door was a barrier between me and the world inside which frightened me.

Don't go inside, don't go in!

You must go in, this is your home.

Don't go in! the voice cried. *Don't go in!*

At last, I was able to move; I had to move, to stand there was to be gripped by nonsensical fears and irrational terror: I must move, get inside, fight down the revolt which battled within me.

Between this house and the next was a narrow service alley, wide enough for a cycle or a barrow but not for a car. In each house wall were small windows; downstairs for the cloakroom, upstairs for the bathroom. Both windows had protective iron bars, of wrought iron — which made them no less like a prison. I hated these bars.

I passed them to the back garden, my heart beating very fast: sickeningly. Had Marcus gone out this way, as he usually did, and left the back door unlocked? Or because I was asleep in the house, had he left it locked and gone out by the front door?

The black iron handle was cold to touch even through gloves. I was almost afraid to turn. The anomaly of the situation came to me: I did not want to go back inside, yet I dreaded the thought of being locked out.

I clutched, and turned, and pushed: and the door opened.

Once inside, with the door closed, I leaned against the sink for what must have been a long time: and I began to shiver. Standing, leaning, shaking, my mind flooded back to the awful attack the night before and what had brought it on. My teeth began to chatter, gently at first, then violently.

Help me!

"Stop it!" I cried aloud. "Stop it!" I forced my body away from the sink, pulled at my gloves, scratched the back of my left hand, tossed the gloves to one side and screamed: "*Stop it, stop it, stop it!*" I made myself move out of the kitchen, and movement helped to steady me, and I would not stop but looked into each room, so spick-and-span and orderly; then went upstairs; holding on to the banister rail, made of black iron, an attempt to make this house appear to be what it was not and could never be: distinctive and attractive in its own right. When I got upstairs my legs were quivering, and tremors ran through my body but the sense of being out of control had gone.

Each room was as I had left it: immaculate.

I crossed to the dressing-table and stood looking at my reflection. I was pale and my eyes were pinky-red at the rims, but there were no outward signs of the conflict which was tearing at me. My handbag was there, on top; it had been within inches of me when I had taken the gloves out of the drawer.

It was a brown calf handbag, a birthday present from Marcus. Under the gentle smoothing of my fingers its quality came through. Although contemporary and mostly Scandinavian inspired, the furniture was all good, too: Marcus would rather go without a thing than buy something of indifferent quality; and everything here was paid for; unlike my father who had never been out of debt, Marcus always paid cash and fought for a discount.

Many women would have considered him an ideal husband, and in some ways he was.

I stared at the double bed; stage of near-tragedy. I could almost hear him in the London shop where he had bought it and several other pieces.

"It must be strong." With a meaning look at me.

"It doesn't matter how wide it is but it must be strong —and firm.

"It mustn't creak.

"My wife will need to be able to push it about easily, for cleaning, but the castors must lock."

And I could hear the voice of the salesman; a faded, grey-haired man: *"Very strong, sir . . . four feet six inches wide . . . very firm, sir . . . These are the new patent castors which lock in position, the bed just has to be raised to release them... Very convenient, sir... very strong, strong, strong..."*

I went into the spare room; where we put our occasional guests; for Marcus had a few relatives, although his friends all lived in the London area and could always get home at night. This room overlooked the back garden; the bathroom and water closet were in between the two rooms. It was not fully furnished yet, just had a single bed, with a folding camp to make a 'twin' in emergency, and a curtain across one corner as a wardrobe, a chest of drawers of pale oak beneath the window with an oval mirror standing on it.

This was not large enough for Marcus; if we were to have separate rooms he must have the other. But did he mean what he said? Would Marcus seriously propose that we should have a room each? And even if he did —

I must go away.

I must go away so that he thought I would come back, but I would never return.

I *had* to leave him; if I didn't I could not be sure what would happen. I only knew one thing for certain: last night had been the last night between us. It would be impossible to tell him so, I had no doubt at all that if I tried he would use force, would subdue me at all costs, if I resisted, would go berserk. I had been wrong in one way last night but I was not wrong about this.

If I packed only a few things —

I *had* only a few things, and I had no money. The little Anthony had left me had gone, and when I had suggested getting a job Marcus had flown into a rage, or else fallen into a mood half-savage, half-sulking. "A man's duty is to keep his wife and family." Period. "If a man cannot earn enough to keep his wife he cannot call himself a man." Period. "A woman's place is in the home." Period. Everything was cut and dried, he would brook no argument. "If you keep this house and look after me properly you will not be lonely." Period.

And one day, fiercely, fingers biting into my shoulders, he had roared:

"I don't want you working with other men, understand? I don't want you being touched — *pawed* — by these lecherous old satyrs. You stay *home*."

Period —

Why did I submit? I often asked myself; but I knew the answer before putting the question. He was too masterful, dominant, all-possessive, and he frightened me.

I lived in fear of him. And I lived in fear of what I would do if I stayed with him.

I dropped on to the side of the spare room bed; it was as solid and firm as the one in the other room. I had no money, could not run away because I had nowhere to go and lacked the courage to walk out. I would be as frightened of the world outside as I would be of him, and of myself. To go would be a futile gesture of defiance.

Help me, help me, help me!

I heard a sound. At first it seemed to come from a long way off: a tapping, but soon I realised that it was from below: a tapping at the front door. Only door-to-door salesmen ever came, or political canvassers, no one in whom I could have the slightest interest. *Go away.* But the tapping went on and suddenly became a loud knocking, as if the caller had been timid at first and suddenly grown bold, banging on the wrought-iron knocker and the wrought-iron plate.

I said, angrily: "Stop it!"

But the knocking was insistent, and I had a sense that the caller would not go away. There were some canvassers so aggressive that they seemed ready to knock the door down, and directly one opened it, thrust a foot inside to make sure they could not have the door slammed on to them.

"Stop it!" I cried, and ran out of the room and down the stairs.

At one time I had been frightened of callers, especially men, but that fear at least had gone, and I would soon send this importunate about his business. I opened the door, mouth open, words on the tip of my tongue.

"What do you mean by — "

The red-haired woman whom I had seen in the street now stood on the path, smiling, yes, smiling and yet giving the impression of embarrassment and timidity; as if she had not a word to say for herself. I had a picture of a pretty, round-faced, freckled woman in a green knitted dress which clung nicely to a youthful figure: but her face wasn't really youthful, she could not be less than forty.

I broke off, feeling foolish.

She gulped, formed words and then uttered them: "Good-good-afternoon."

What could I say but a stiff: "Good afternoon."

"I — hope I'm not bothering you." She was American, I realised; or at least she spoke with an American accent. Her eyes were both gold and green in colour, and not at all timid.

"What do you want?" I asked ungraciously.

"I — I wondered if you could spare me some sugar," she said, with an apologetic smile.

"Sugar?" I echoed, in surprise.

"Yes, I — we — can't find any. We — we've just moved in."

"Oh!" I exclaimed. "Two or three doors along."

"That's right," she answered. "The moving men have just gone and I was making some coffee for me and my husband when I discovered that I had mislaid the sugar.

I tried the neighbours on either side of me but there was
no one in, I guess. If I've disturbed you — "

"Not at all," I made myself say. "I'll get some — but
do come in."

"Why, thank you!" The pretty face lit up.

She carried a large, red enamel mug in her left hand,
which clashed with her own colouring, but I did not notice
that as I led the way to the kitchen. Marcus having a
sweet tooth there is always plenty of sugar, and instead of
taking a canister from the shelf I opened the larder door.
The kitchens in Dingle Park houses are spacious, being
meant for families, and there was ample storage space for
a family of two. I took down a two-pound bag of granu-
lated sugar, and said:

"Why don't you take this — you'll be able to last for a
day or two then."

"You're very kind," she said, and laughed. "I was told
the English would be so stand-offish, I hardly dared to
bother you."

Something struck me as false about that statement —
after all she *hadn't* been hesitant. But at the moment I did
not dwell on it nor allow it to trouble me. I felt an almost
irresistible urge to talk to her, to say anything to make
her stay, to tell her that I dreaded being in this house alone,
that unexpected and at first unwelcome as she had been she
was a gift from heaven, so — natural, easy talking, surely
easy to talk to. And I longed to talk but with the longing
was fear of what would happen if I did; fear that she would
scoff at my fears or at best make light of them. And how
could I talk to, confide in, a total stranger?

I knew that I could not.

At last, I said in a husky voice: "It's no bother at all—
is there anything else you would like?"

"No," she replied, slowly. "You're very kind. May I

come and bother you again if I find I'm out of something else?"

"Of course," I said. "Have you — have you bought the house?"

"Oh, no," she answered. "We've just rented it. George, my husband, is here in England for one year. He will be working at Starfills." She stopped, as if expecting me to say that I knew Starfills, but when I didn't answer she went on lightly: "That's the new factory where they make toy stars and displays. Does your husband work on the estate, also?"

"Oh, no," I answered. "In the city."

"The city?" She looked puzzled. "The city of London?"

"It's *the* city of London," I said, and seeing how baffled she seemed I laughed and went on lightly: "When you've settled in you must come and have some tea — or coffee!" I laughed again, "and I'll try to explain. Not that I'm an expert on the city of London, I was brought up in the country."

"You were!" she exclaimed. "How about that! I'm a country girl myself, but George — " She broke off, and looked away from me for the first time, holding the sugar to her bosom and dangling the red mug from her thumb. "Honey, I must go or George will wonder what has happened to me. I surely am grateful." She turned towards the narrow passage, moving with greater freedom, and went on over her shoulder: "Our name is Jees. Isn't that awful?"

"Jees," I echoed.

"J-E-E-S," she spelled out, half-laughing, and turning round as if to judge my reaction to the name.

"I don't think it's awful at all," I said. "Our name is Hunter."

"Mrs. Hunter, I feel very happy at having you for a

neighbour," Mrs. Jees said lightly, and for the first time she sounded slightly embarrassed. "I imagine it's too early to start calling each other by our first names. We would do that in America — "

"I'm Janetta Hunter," I told her.

"Janetta! Why, that's an unusual name!"

"I think my father invented it," I said, feeling much lighter-hearted than I had for a long, long time.

"I wish mine had been more inventive," she said. "I'm just plain American Esmé — Esmé Jees, four E's!" I did not follow that last remark but there was something so light-hearted about her, an infectious gaiety which lifted my spirits long after she had left, hurrying then because she had stayed so long and her George would wonder what had happened to her. I actually began to hum to myself, something I had not done for a long time.

Then, I stopped: as if I had been struck a savage blow.

I could 'see' Esmé Jees's bright face and eager eyes and 'hear' her light, lively voice, but until this moment I had not realised that she had lied to me about her reason for coming. She must surely have lied. No one who felt timid in a new country would bang on the door of a strange house so thunderously just because she wanted to borrow some sugar.

5

Spy or Neighbour?

WHY ON EARTH SHOULD SHE HAVE LIED? I ASKED MYSELF
time and time again.

No answer presented itself, no explanation, but the conclusion was clear; after each examination of what had
happened it seemed clearer. No one would have gone to
such trouble for a few ounces of sugar — why, there were
shops at the entrance to the estate and Esmé Jees could
not have reached this street without passing them. She had
lied to me and I could not understand why, unless —

Unless she was spying on me. Nonsense! I cried within
myself. Why should she spy? Why should anyone, if it
came to that — any neighbour, above all one who had
moved in only this day.

Why should anyone spy?

There was an answer: the question was not as hollow
as it sounded. Marcus *might* have employed, or used, some
neighbour to tell him whenever I left the house, where I
went, when I came back. It would not surprise me if he
did: I was virtually certain that he had done so before, but
— this woman, an American whom he could not know.
That wasn't possible!

Could he?

I thought of neighbours, few of whom I knew more than
to say 'good morning' or 'goodnight'. The few who had

made overtures soon after we had come here had been rebuffed. "Common louts," Marcus had called them. "We don't want to mix with such people, Janetta. Do you understand?"

I understood.

"There's no need to be rude to them; you can put them off politely."

So it had been 'I'm sorry, I'm sorry, I'm sorry' to every invitation to a drink; coffee; a party; Christmas, New Year, any celebration. The neighbours on our left were middle-aged and both worked 'in the city'. The neighbours on our right both worked, the father in one of the factories on the industrial estate, the mother in a works canteen, from which she came home just in time to meet her three boisterous children, two boys and a girl; apart from an occasional 'good morning' or 'good evening' over the fence at the back I had hardly seen them.

"It's far better to keep ourselves to ourselves, Janetta."

Was *he* afraid that if I came to know any of the neighbours too well, I would talk of his — excesses? The very thought was obscene! But there were families in the street, Henley Street, with whom he had talked occasionally, whom I believed he might use to watch me. But not this new American family, the Jees. It simply wasn't thinkable.

Then why had she come with such insistence?

And why had she been just outside the gate when I had gone out that afternoon? I remembered her now, the sun touching her hair with vivid fire. She had been approaching slowly when I had gone out and turned and almost run towards Dingle Park and the few hours of false freedom.

There was nothing to stop me from going out now.

I had my bag. It was not yet three o'clock. There was time to do a lot of shopping between now and six o'clock, when I must be home, for Marcus. He would be in at half-past six and would want to eat at seven o'clock. To-night's meal was no problem: I would cook steaks and have chips ready to drop into the boiling oil; and there was a variety of frozen green vegetables, he always liked to make his own choice.

Why had Esmé Jees lied to me?

Was she watching me now?

The thought took my breath away, and without waiting I went upstairs to the main bedroom and went to the window, on the right-hand side, keeping close to the wall so that no one passing could glance up and see me. The van had gone, of course, but there was a small, green-coloured Italian car outside the gate of the house where the Jees had moved, and I had not seen such a car there before. No one was in the tiny garden and the few people in the street showed no interest in their house or mine.

Mine? Or Marcus's? Everything here belonged to Marcus; only my personal belongings, none of great value, were mine. I had been so — impoverished when I had married him. Poor — and lonely — and bereft. After — after — after Anthony had been murdered.

My teeth began to chatter and my body began to shake. Thinking back consciously to the manner of Anthony's death always affected me like that: on a lesser key I felt as I had last night, in convulsions, in a paroxysm of fear of some unknown or unrealised thing.

I did not want to think about Anthony. I did not want to think.

I wanted to leave this place and run and keep on running until I was far away from the world I knew, far from my own fears, from memory. From the questions the police had asked, unending questions with unending patience and with unending scepticism. Never a deliberate:

"We do not — I *do* not — believe you," just the questions asked over and over again in a flat and unemotional voice.

"When did you last see your husband?"

"Did you know that he was seeing another woman?"

"Did you know he had a mistress?"

"Do you know who bought him the chocolates?"

"But he was your husband. You must have known he liked chocolates."

"Did he ever buy you any chocolates?... He did?... Were they always the same make? If so, what make?... Are you sure they weren't always the same make or brand?"

"Surely you knew how much he relished chocolates."

"Did he have a sweet tooth for other things?... Ah, Turkish Delight ... And crystallised fruits, yes."

"To get back to the subject of chocolates, how often did you buy him a box of Alconut brand?... The chocolate with ... Very well, Mrs. Grey, I have noted your answer, I assure you there is no need to shout ... You state categorically that you did not at any time buy a box of Alconut chocolates ... I beg your pardon?... You cannot remember having bought such a brand, that is a somewhat different story."

"Mrs. Grey — you know that your husband died as a result of eating chocolates which contained — as well as the ingredients of the sweetmeat itself — sufficient arsenic to have killed several people. Oh, dear! Can we get you some water, Mrs. Grey? Or a little whisky or brandy?"

No, no, no, no!

I never drank alcohol, have never drunk alcohol ...

Then have some tea, Mrs. Grey?... Milk?... And sugar?

Sugar!

Someone had lied to me this day about sugar, or

someone had lied about the reason for coming to see me. Why should she lie? What point could there possibly be in lying? But she had lied and I wanted to know why, had to know why.

What would she say if I went and asked her? Would she admit to lying and have a reason, or would she scoff at me with a bold-faced 'no'? What else could she do? What possible use was there in trying to make her tell me?

"Mrs. Grey?" The policeman was a grey-haired, benign-looking man, whose name I had not remembered for a long time. "Do you insist that you did not know there were two unopened packets of Alconut chocolates, the flat pack which fits into a pocket or a handbag so easily, in your husband's desk?"

"I tell you I didn't know!"

"And you did not know that Alconut chocolates was a brand he often bought for office snacks?"

"No, I tell you. No, no, no!"

"How a wife could live with her husband and not know such a significant fact — "

"I didn't know, he didn't tell me, he didn't eat chocolates when we were at home!"

In one way, those awful days of the inquest seemed a long way off; an illimitable way back in time, and it was almost as if they had never been. In another way it was like yesterday. Anthony, not Marcus; Anthony away all day and often home late at night. After working late. "I'm sorry, dear, I couldn't do anything about it." Who told me that? Anthony or Marcus? Whose voice did I hear? Anthony's or Marcus's? Who was lying to me? Which husband was the liar?

Anthony's lies mattered.

Anthony, coming home with lipstick on his collar; with

the scent of another woman's powder on his face, his clothes, his handkerchief. Anthony spending precious money, our money, on some whore of a woman, so that he had died in debt. Oh, how I hated Anthony's lies, Anthony's deceits, Anthony's hypocrisy, and the loneliness he caused me. The alone-ness. The long dead hours by myself, with only one relief from the dreariness, one way to drown my sorrows, to ease my pain.

The piano. The lovely white keys and the beautiful sound; the majesty of the crescendo and the beauty of the tinkling notes; the gentleness and the hardness, the ripple as of laughter and the shouting as of hate. This was music I could make myself; not create, never a note which some master had not struck as with a master-key, but music I could strike out of the wooden box and from the taut strings. Music which could transcend both love and hate, which sometimes replaced both love and hate.

"I'm sorry, sweetheart, I had to stay late again."

"Did you, dear?"

"Couldn't get out of it, I'm afraid."

"They make you work too hard."

Hypocrite, mockery, hypocrite — but how much better to be such a hypocrite, to pretend I did not know that he was lying, than to make the lies myself.

"Did you play tonight?"

"Yes, a little."

"What did you play?"

As if he cared, as if it mattered — except that any play-ing seemed to him to atrophy my mind; seemed, to him, an abstract substitute for his so splendid body. Hypocrite! Liar!

"Rachmaninoff," I might say. Or "Tchaikovsky," or . . . And that was all he wanted; a familiar name, seen on gramophone records or on programmes or heard on the radio spoken by men whose voices could be a kind of music or could be stiff and artificial: like a ventriloquist's dummy.

"Tired, dear?"

He meant, *he* was tired, worn out, exhausted.

"I am rather."

In minutes he would be asleep. For hours, I would lie awake.

One night, which I remembered with as much horror as I remembered the subsequent nightmare events, I lay and watched him: and for the first time a thought crossed my mind.

Kill him, kill him, kill him, kill him! It was like a screeching horror, splitting my brain.

I made myself some tea, ate some biscuits and a sandwich, was hungrier than I had realised and made myself some toast and scrambled some eggs. I felt much better. I knew what had been going through my mind but it no longer shocked me. I faced a simple truth.

I had wanted to kill Anthony, because he had lied and deceived me, taken money which should have been mine and spent it on others. Oh, I had loved him, wanted and desired him, but the day had come when I knew he would never be mine again, that he stayed with me only because his true love, his mistress, was married to a man who would not divorce her; and because his true love, his mistress, had three children, one a child of less than six months. A child conceived when Anthony had known her; probably, his child.

I could kill him!

Soon, Marcus would be home.

The hours had dragged but this half-hour would fly. I

had to make up my mind about so many things, and he would want to know what I had decided to do, *if* he was in the same frame of mind. I had known him in good and understanding moods, sympathetic and prepared to help me, and I had known such moods snap like a too-taut string. I believed that even if he had meant all he had said last night he would expect me to have decided which course to take.

I could go away — for as long as he would let me.

I could make up the spare room as mine and leave 'ours' to him.

I could see a doctor.

Oh, nonsense! What use would a doctor be in such a problem as this. I did not need and would not see a doctor!

The oil for the chips was heating, giving off a faint odour. The steak, beaten on the wooden board, was smeared with butter and ready for the grill; a large steak for him and small for me: that was my choice.

Very soon, he would be here.

I began to panic. There was no reason in me, no sense at all, I had lost all self-control. I should have run away, I should never have come back. Even if I had come back I should have collected my handbag and packed a few clothes and gone again.

It was madness to think he would really let me go, even for a few days. He would be here any minute.

I must be calm; be normal; behave as if nothing had happened. No matter what his mood *I must keep calm.* And I must look my best. Goodness! I flew upstairs and put on a little lipstick, the merest trace of rouge and powder, and ran a comb through my thick, dark hair. Except that I was breathing too shallowly I was normal enough, and I must go downstairs slowly, check everything in the kitchen, go out into the square box of a front room with its angular chairs which looked so uncomfortable yet had a most seductive ease.

Please God, he would be in a good mood when he came. Not sneering; not telling me as he often did that I talked in my sleep and had admitted killing Anthony.

Please God, he would help, not drive me to distraction.

Please God, I would not wish him dead.

The moment came when his key turned in the lock of the front door.

6

Homecoming

"WELL," MARCUS SAID. "HAVE YOU DECIDED WHAT TO DO?"

In the tautness of his lips, the almost imperceptible strain at his eyes, even in the tone of his voice, was the evidence that all was not well. There was evidence of tensions he had suffered during the day and of the effort he was making now. If I vacillated, he would lose his self-control, begin to shout at me, to rave: I was as sure of that as I was sure that I was sitting on a low stool in front of him, in the front room.

We had finished dinner in a mood of dangerous politeness.

"Yes, dear. Thank you, dear. Really? What was your day like? There are some Americans next door but two. Really? The woman came and asked if I could spare some sugar. Then she can't be very efficient. I suppose not, dear."

Now, he was sitting at ease, with his back to the window. It was still broad daylight. More people were in the street including a bunch of teenagers on bicycles; the Bells, in the house opposite, were sitting in the garden, reading the evening papers. Coffee was on a small table between us, a tall green pot, tall green cups.

"Well? Have you decided what to do?"

"It isn't easy," I said.

"From the way you behaved last night I would have thought that any alternative was better for you than the present situation."

I could be humble; submit to his hectoring. That was what I always did. It was what he expected. Except that the disturbance had gone deeper and in me was more profound, last night had been no different from other nights. Oh: and except that he had appeared to be more deeply affected and anxious to make amends; at least, to help.

He was beginning to frown; anger was rising because I did not utter some placatory word. I knew what he really wanted, what he would try to get: an apology, an admission that the fault was wholly mine, that he was as blameless as a saint. Perhaps it was the moods which had swept through me during the day, the spirit of revolt, which made me hesitate.

"*Well!* Can't you say *some*thing?" He sat more upright in his chair.

Out of the blue and surprising me as much as it surprised him, I said quite calmly:

"I'm not sure that any of the alternatives is the right solution, Marcus."

"Oh," he said, his teeth nearly clenched. "You aren't." His nostrils began to distend, too. Yet in his way he was so handsome; so brutally male-looking.

"No," I said.

"Then perhaps in the solitude of the house I have provided for you, you have thought of another alternative."

"Yes," I answered.

"Am I to be allowed to hear it?"

I knew what I was going to suggest; realised that it had been buried in my sub-conscious all the time — had perhaps never really gone away. That didn't surprise me:

what surprised me was my calmness, and the ease with
which I spoke, the fact that I could so easily read the
symptoms of a rising tumult but was not afraid; was not
near-suffocated by the thumping of my heart as I usually
was when I defied him.

"Marcus," I said, "there's no need to be so pompous."

"Pompous!"

"Would you like some more coffee?"

"Pompous!"

"That's right," I said, still calmly; but now he gripped
the wooden arms of his chair, and any moment might
spring to his feet. "That is exactly how you are behaving,
dear. Would you like some more coffee?"

"No, I would not!"

"Then I'll take the coffee things out and — " I began
to get up.

"Stay there!" he rasped; there was no other word to
describe the sound of his voice, it was as if he were trying
to imprison a roar of anger. "I want to talk to you."

Here was a climax. I could sit back and do what he said,
or I could go ahead and do what I had said I meant to do.
For the first time I felt a flood of uneasiness; fear. But I
also felt something else: awareness that if I allowed myself
to be shouted into submission my incipient revolt would
be crushed and rendered futile. It took a great deal of
effort, but, still looking at him, I stood up. I have always
taken great pleasure in my ease of movement; my flexi-
bility; and now whatever the mental there was no physical
effort.

"Marcus," I said, "you really must stop treating me as
if I were a child."

He sprang to his feet, flung out one arm, gripped my
forearms as I reached for the coffee tray; and his grip
was powerful enough to hurt.

"Do what you're told! Stay there."

He tried to force me to sit down, and of course he could do so if he exerted a tithe of his strength. Anger flashed from his eyes, his lips were parted and his nostrils so distended that he looked really ugly.

I said exactly what I thought.

"Let me go, at once. You look like a beast on the rampage."

He was so astounded that he relaxed his grip; so astounded that he could not use his favourite trick when he wanted to gain time: roar one or two of the words I had used in a frightening echo.

I freed myself, placed his cup and saucer on the tray, and rose with the tray in my hands. He could have stopped me but did not move until I was in the passage, making myself walk steadily. Now my heart was beginning to thump, because I did not know what would happen if he followed me. I knew what *might* happen. He would set out to prove his absolute mastery, and to him mastery over a woman meant, ultimately, only one thing.

I reached the kitchen and placed the coffee things in the sink, already filled with the other dishes and knives and forks and a strong detergent solution. I expected to hear him come after me, but he did not, and there was no point in delaying the issue: I could not refuse to face it now. So I wiped my hands and went along the passage. He had moved to the window, and was looking out, both hands deep in his trousers pockets. He might possibly pretend that he did not know I was in the room, so I moved a chair with enough noise to make sure he heard, and then sat down in it. This was a chair without arms, the 'mother' chair to his 'father's' chair and it was on the opposite side of the small fireplace.

He spoke without turning round.

"What is your additional alternative?"

"That I should go out to work," I said.

"You know what I think of that."

"It is my life we are discussing Marcus — what I need to do."

"Your duty is here." Still he did not turn round.

"Spending all my time in this little place isn't right," I said.

"It is your home. Your duty is — "

"Marcus," I interrupted, "for as long as we are together it *is* my duty to look after the house and see that you get well-fed and your creature comforts are not neglected. That I shall do. But I don't have enough to do here during the day, and going away for a few weeks, or even having my own bedroom, won't be enough in itself. But I'm sure you're right and we should have separate rooms. I shall move my things to the small room, and — "

"*What* did you say?" he interrupted.

I had said so many things but the last of any significance was that we should have separate rooms. I thought that was what struck fire: what made him swing round, glaring at me as if he thought that his expression alone could frighten me into submission. Now that I had made that decision I must stick to it.

"It was your suggestion, and — "

"Did you say 'for as long as we are together'?"

I was startled, that the effect of that should have been so long delayed, but had no doubt that it had gored into him like a sword in a wound already there.

"Yes," I said.

"Are you contemplating leaving me?"

"Not yet," I said, "but — "

"Don't lie to me!" He took a step nearer.

"No, I am not at this moment contemplating leaving you," I answered, "but we cannot go on living together as we have in the past months. You must know that as well as I."

He took another step, and was only a few feet away. He seemed to fight to get words out, but at last they came.

"Who is he?"

I was astounded. "Don't be silly, there isn't — "

"Who is he?" Now he raised his hands and the fingers were crooked as if he would love to clamp them about my throat. Fear began to tear at the calmness which had remained with me so blessedly long, for he was between me and the door.

I had begun to think of running away from him.

"There is no other man."

"You're lying to me. There must be a man. Who is he?"

"Marcus — " I began.

"If you don't tell me who he is I'll choke the life out of you," he said in a growling voice. "There must be a man. You could never think of leaving me if there wasn't someone else who would take care of you. It wouldn't even enter your head. *Who — is — the — man?*"

It was useless to go on denying the existence of a man with words.

I could not get out of the room; he would hold me. If I were to break this sudden, frightening tension I would have to find a different way, would have first to shock and even frighten him, and I did not know whether I could do either.

I said: "If you lay a hand on me, I shall leave this house and never come back."

For a moment I thought I had shocked him enough; made him feel that whatever drastic step I took would be caused by his behaviour. He actually drew back. As the immediate danger receded, my heart began to beat much faster, and sickeningly; the release from tension had also brought the release of the fear stored up inside me.

Then he said in a strange and strangled voice, a tortured voice:

"I'll teach you where you belong."

He seized me.

He flung me over his shoulder as if I were a half-filled sack.

He took me to 'our' room.

He tore off my clothes —

I opened my eyes and looked up into his face and there was only one thought in my mind.

To kill him.

He said: "You stay here. You do what I tell you. If ever you run away with anyone I'll find you and bring you back. I'll hunt you to the ends of the earth. You belong to me and here you will stay."

It was quiet; very quiet. He was not snoring, for once. At least now, I was alone. He had ravaged me and threatened me and now he had cast me off. This was, with less violence, the pattern of our life, and there was no hope of changing the pattern. He meant exactly what he said and by meaning it, by his demonstration of his mastery, he was confident that he could subdue me.

Now, spent, I lay absolutely still. Even my mind was spent and I could think little more than I could feel.

I felt hopeless and helpless, and yet — there *was* a stirring of hope in me.

There must have been or surely I would not have slept.

When I woke, I heard a sound I had not heard in this house: the sound of a piano being played, clearly, brightly, beautifully. It was Chopin's *Prelude in C Minor*. The notes came as if from the room below me, floating through the window. At first, they brought balm to me; quiet and contentment.

I knew that piece so well, had played it so often. To —

Anthony. The name sliced through me, like a knife stroke; seemed to cleave my head in two. Anthony.

I was dreaming, there was no piano here, this was dream turning into nightmare. A voice was superimposed upon the music, the pleasant, deep, authoritative voice of the policeman who had questioned me so exhaustively after Anthony's death.

"*Did you buy your husband chocolates?*"

"No."

"*Did you know he liked a certain brand of nut milk chocolates called Alconut very much?*"

"No, I didn't know."

"*Come, Mrs. Grey — you lived with your husband day in, day out. How could he have kept such a little domestic thing from you?*"

"I tell you I didn't know."

"*I think you must have known!*"

"I did not."

"*He actually kept some of these in his desk.*"

"I never looked in his desk."

I had never looked in Anthony's desk — at least, not until the end of his life. It was an unwritten law: what was his was his, what was mine was mine. Each was his own, inviolate. But had I looked I might have seen the letters which would have told me about her: about Hilary. About the end of our love. I had learned of this cruelly, in a letter which had slipped into the lining of a jacket he asked me to repair. I had run my hands round to find if anything was inside, and there had been one brief note, all I needed for proof.

I had played to him so often.

In the early days, when he had been reading or working at home, I would play and he would love to have the music in the background. "It soothes me and makes my mind work better." Afterwards I had played to the empty room, the empty house: or sometimes, at a weekend when I had him captive because his Hilary had her other life to care for, I would play in desperation; pleadingly; but all to no effect.

Now, I heard it from the past.

I screwed up my eyes but the sound still came: sounds I loved but had learned to hate.

Hate.

Nonsense!

I opened my eyes. The sun was bright outside and against a corner of the window, so the morning was well advanced: ten o'clock, perhaps. There were street noises and there was this pure music. It was not from my past, no nightmare: it was being made now as I had so often made it. Not from the room below but from along the street.

Suddenly, I knew who was making it.

I lay still, on my side, listening; soothed now that the early association had faded from my mind: loving the lilting beauty. And whoever played, played well; here and there a false note, a wrong emphasis, but most of the time it was pure delight. It was almost certainly Esmé Jees, of course — unless it was her husband. No one else in the street played music — *real* music. I sensed that it was the woman, and remembered she had come to see me and had lied about the sugar.

Had she lied? Or had I simply thought so in the intensity of my fears? Now she was playing the music with which I had first wooed and won, then despairingly lost, my Anthony. Whom I had loved. *And* killed?

7

Second Day

WHILE I WAS DRESSING THE MUSIC STOPPED, AND ALL I
could hear was the drone of the milkman's electric cart
moving along the street. I felt suddenly deserted; more
alone than on waking. I wished she would start playing
again, wanted to lean out of the window and call to her;
instead, amid the silence, I went downstairs. The kitchen
was exactly as it had been yesterday morning; Marcus had
used the same dishes and knives and spoons for the same
coffee and cereal.

What had his mood been?

Had he felt the slightest remorse or compunction? Did
it occur to him for a moment that by behaving so he was
killing the last spark of hope there was of a life between
us?

Had he the faintest idea of what had passed through my
mind as I had stared up at him and he had laboured in
man's nearest approach to giving birth?

What an awful thing it would be if I had a child from
such an onslaught?

I actually laughed; a weak, helpless little giggle but
nevertheless a laugh, for if I had ever been going to
have a child, I would not be lonely now. In those first two
golden years with Anthony . . .

His voice came to me, as out of a mist.

"I love you, Janetta."

"And I love you."

"Will you always love me?"

"Always. But will *you* always love *me*?"

He had taken my hand, and I could remember his words as if they had been spoken yesterday. "For ever and ever, my darling, for ever and ever."

And his tone was so sincere, his hand so firm on mine, who could have disbelieved him?

Brave words to say to a woman born to be barren: *For ever and ever, my darling, for ever and ever*. I shivered, yet still laughed. It was macabre to think back, and I had to laugh or I would have given myself up to an orgy of weeping, because I would have remembered all the time of waiting and hoping, the slow dying of hope, the understanding that I was losing Anthony because of the fact that I could not give him a child. Oh, it was a fact. I saw doctor after doctor and took drug after drug; it was a fact.

It was not Anthony.

Anthony was already a father, but his children were now in Australia with their grandparents. But what he had done, with whom he had been before we met, was not my concern; was no cause for anguish.

What an awful thing, if I had a child by Marcus.

I began to giggle again but stopped almost at once. There was no humour left in the situation, the very possibility was revolting.

To have a child by him might be to have a child like him.

I would rather kill myself.

There, then, was the answer to all my problems, and this was not the first time I had become aware of it. But in the past I had never dwelt on the ways in which I could kill myself. Now, I began to, almost with eagerness and certainly with relief. How? Poison — but how would I get the drugs? Aspirins — yes, I could buy aspirins and enough would kill me. Arsenic — as Anthony had died. Awful, awful. Arsenic, from a weed-killer, and Marcus was a fanatic about the garden, hating weeds as if they were human beings. Drown? Would it be easy to drown? To make oneself stay under water? I could swim, a little, I would probably try to save myself. To jump in front of a car? And so leave a scar on the mind of the driver? No — far better a train, where the driver was more remote. Jump from a high window or a high bridge on to the line.

I stood in the kitchen as these possibilities passed through my mind. I heard a train.

I knew what it was, of course; the familiar distant rumble which grew louder as the train drew nearer the embankment which was only a few hundred yards away. Often, one was aware of the oncoming, the passing and the disappearing train without it disturbing one's thoughts, or even considering what it was; but now I listened, and the *t'rump-t'rump, thump, thump, t'rump-t'rump, thump, thump* of the train wheels over the joints in the rails began to keep pace with the beating of my heart. *T'rump-t'rump, thump, thump, t'rump-t'rump, thump, thump.* The window was open because of the warmth of the morning, and the wind was blowing this way, so that the sound was louder. Wheels and heart, beating together; wheels and heart, throbbing together.

The train noise faded into the distance. The noise of my beating heart seemed to possess my body and fill the room.

It would be so easy. First, a short climb, not much farther than I had climbed yesterday. It would not be particularly noticeable, either, for people did climb up to the top of the embankment for the view beyond; a view over all of London, when on a fine day one could see the distant environs and the far-off green countryside.

There were steps, cut into the grass-soil by generations of children and their parents; of young lovers, seeking to hide by night; of the many who wanted simply to see the view.

T'rump-t'rump, thump, thump; t'rump-t'rump, thump, thump.

Yes, it would be so easy, for trains passed over the body so quickly.

In the winter or the autumn —

But this was high summer, and it could not wait.

It would be so easy.

Why not *now*?

If I killed myself today I would never see Marcus again, never undergo such ravaging, never know such hopelessness or experience such fear. It would be over. Like sleep. I would — my muscles tensed and my heart shrank at the thought — I would have to key myself up for the final moment, there would be an instant of crunching pain, but after that — oblivion.

No fear or dread.

No abuses.

No memories and no doubts.

Oblivion.

And who else would suffer? Marcus? Even as I asked myself that question I almost laughed. He would miss me as one might miss a slave. My mother and my father were long since dead: if there were an afterlife they would surely welcome me. Two sisters, each of whom lived half-a-world away.

No one would actually be hurt, and I would stop hurting.

Was it — cowardly?

Nothing could be more cowardly than the life I led; from which I dared not even run away.

Supposing — supposing I *did* run away? Where would I go and what could I live on? With money from Marcus I could exist, but without it I could not exist for a week. I had not worked for so long that the welfare agencies would have nothing for me. I might try for work as I would have had last night's discussion gone differently, but what could I do? Help in a house? Care for children and weep inwardly for those of my own whom I could not have? Work in a shop?

Wherever I went, Marcus would find me.

If I were gone for more than a few days he would tell the police that I was missing and would have them search for me. And if I went back, no matter what glib assurances he gave me and gave the authorities, then he would punish me; subordinate me in every way he could.

Why wasn't it easy to walk out of his life?

Why wasn't it as easy to leave him as it was to walk up the railway embankment and fling oneself in front of a train?

Why did I keep saying 'oneself'? Why didn't I tell the simple truth . . . 'and fling myself in front of a train'?

Why couldn't I just walk out on Marcus?

Why was it so much easier to kill myself than to kill him?

Why must I be the one who wanted to kill?

"Did you give your husband those chocolates knowing he would eat them and die?"

"No, I did not."

"Did you buy those chocolates?"

"No, I did not."

"Did you know your husband was having an *affaire* with another woman?"

"No, I did not."

But that was a lie, a deliberate lie. I knew that if I admitted knowing about Hilary then there would be a motive for me to kill Anthony; unless I knew there was no motive at all. This much was certain. I had read of a similar situation not once but a hundred, sometimes it seemed a thousand times, for it was stock-in-mind of every writer whose mystery stories helped to fill the shelves of the library in Hendleton, and the Mobile Branch when it came to Dingle Park and stood for half-a-day outside the dozen small shops which served the district and the industrial estate. So often there was nothing to do but read, and so many of these were so easy to read.

A murderer must have a motive.

"Were you aware that this association between your husband and Hilary Consett had been going on for nearly two years?"

"I didn't know it was going on at all."

"You mean you had no suspicion at all?"

"Of course I hadn't!" I had cried. "I loved my husband, I trusted him!"

Gay, handsome, lying deceiver. Anthony, if only you were alive today, then I would know where to come, then I would know who would give me help. Married to me or married to her, you would help me because your heart is kind. You could have a dozen mistresses, a hundred *affaires*, if only you were alive today I would not care. I would play for you and wait for you and love you and hope for a little love in return but the most important thing would be that you were here, back in this world from which some human being drove you.

"Did you buy him these chocolates, Mrs. Grey?"

"No, no, no, no."

"Did you get them from his desk and put the poison in them?"

"*No!*"

"It was easy to do; just melt a little of the chocolate, make a hole in the bottom with a hot darning needle, or a knitting needle, put in the poison and seal the hole with melted chocolate. Do you see how easy it would be?"

"Yes, yes, but I didn't do it!"

Could I be sure?

Could I remember all I did and said and threatened?

I knew about Hilary and his love for her.

I did not know that he kept chocolates in his desk.

What did I know and what had I forgotten?

Who had killed beloved Anthony?

Had I?

Was that why when I thought of my hatred of Marcus, my thoughts turned only to ways and means by which to kill him?

Or, to kill myself?

What was the truth?

One thing was certain, I told myself: I could not go on for there would be no peace now, wherever I was.

I knew at last why I stayed with Marcus, why I had not run away and forged a new life for myself. I dared not, because wherever I went I would be haunted by fear of what I might have done. Here, at times, I could forget. Hating Marcus and suffering at his hands and by his body I could forget how much I had come to hate Anthony, or at least, how much I thought I had hated him.

I knew why I stayed: it was a penance because of what I had thought about Anthony the Beloved, but —

Had I killed Anthony?

I did not know.

Did I, truly, want to know?

Had not the time come to give up all knowledge and all hope, by going freely and alone, out of this world?

T'rump-t'rump, thump, thump; t'rump-t'rump, thump, thump.

Should I leave a note for Marcus? Or for the police? Or both?

Why?

When they found me they would want to know why I had killed myself, and they would question him. Let them ask him a thousand questions, as the police had questioned me. Let him hear them talk together as I had once heard the Superintendent who had questioned me talk to another, who had asked:

"Do you believe her?"

"I am inclined to. She sticks to her story."

"But it still doesn't make sense."

"That she didn't know about the other woman — nonsense," 'my' man had said. "In half the happy marriages the wife doesn't know how much she owes to the other woman."

"But not to know about the chocolates — "

"He might have kept them from his wife because his Hilary bought them ... I tell you, you can't even begin to guess what goes on in the mind of your closest friend. Even Manny Cellini doesn't pretend to know."

"But he often seems to," the other rejoined.

I could imagine Marcus being questioned.

"But surely you knew your wife was unhappy ... Any woman driven to take her own life must be in a terrible state of mind ... Were you on good terms ... Did you quarrel very often? ... *Never?*" I could imagine the scepticism he would put into his voice when he uttered that single word. "Mr. Hunter, did you ever strike your wife?... Use any form of violence?... We are puzzled because of the bruises — "

There would be no bruises!

There would be so little of me left whole.

T'rump-t'rump, thump, thump.

8

Hurry, Hurry

WELL? HAVE YOU DECIDED WHAT TO DO?

I was hectoring myself in the way that Marcus did so often; giving myself no peace. But the truth, of course, was that there was no peace.

It was at least three weeks since I had first thought seriously of suicide, sometimes remembering vividly, sometimes shuddering at the thought. There had been a kind of armistice between Marcus and me, most of the time; he had even taken me out, once to a West End theatre, once to a film — *Dr. Zhivago*, which we had never seen — at Hendleton. During these periods life was bearable, but something built up in Marcus and eventually exploded.

He had lost all self-control again last night, and everything was crowding back into my mind.

I sat on the side of the big, the strong, the firm bed, and looked at myself in the cross-shaped mirror. My eyes were a deeper red than they had been and one was slightly bloodshot, but I would have been satisfied, usually; there was at least an appearance of calm, almost of serenity.

"Well?" I spoke aloud. "Have you decided what to do?"

"Yes," I answered into the mirror, and I was quite sure that I had.

"*Are* you quite certain?"

"I am absolutely certain."

"And what are you going to do?"

"I am going to throw myself in front of a train," I answered.

A third voice from somewhere inside me seemed to say: "Well done. No tremor in the voice, no change of expression. You really do have yourself under control."

I asked, loudly: "When are you going to do this thing?"

"Today. Now. At least I am going to set out now."

And I nodded to myself as if to allay all doubts; and the mirror reflection nodded back.

I examined myself more closely, then took out a lipstick and touched up my lips; a compact, and powdered my cheeks and nose.

"You'll do," I said aloud, and almost laughed.

The relief was enormous, like the lifting of a huge weight. And my mood did not change as I went downstairs, clasping my handbag. I made sure all the gas taps in the kitchen were turned off, then went out by the front door. I was in the street with the houses behind me when I realised that I was leaving for the last time, and had no desire to look back. There was no note; no goodbye; Marcus would come home and find the house empty and because for a while he would think I had defied him and run away, he would storm and rave.

Or would he, with no one to impress or to frighten?

A strange thought entered my mind: that I might know, that I might be able to see. It was not that I was a believer but so many were.

I did not look back.

Several people were in their gardens, only a few were in the streets. Most of the benches in the park were occupied with old men, nodding; and two of them, talking. Reminiscing? I wondered. Or boasting of the deeds of youth or even the days of their virility.

The sun was warm and life-giving. The birds were everywhere, and never still: revelling in life. The insects hummed and used every second of their short and measured days.

A youngish-looking man whom I knew slightly as a neighbour to nod to, came from a clump of the older oak, with a Dalmatian dog on a long leash. The dog looked up at me and sniffed and turned his head; the man smiled and said: "Good morning. It's a fine morning." He was the man of the American couple who had moved into the nearby house three weeks ago. I had often seen them out together and remembered his name — George Jees — as well as hers, Esmé's.

It was not until I was a hundred yards away from him that I realised he had spoken more like an Englishman than an American, but I did not look back. Nevertheless I carried a picture of him as I walked up the hill towards the steps worn in the embankment; a youngish-looking man with fair hair, rather curly and bushy but not long in the hippy style. He wore a dark blue shirt and a pair of tight trousers: jeans. And the dog had been sniffing at the air as if finding life good.

So did I.

Fear and doubt and mistrust and self-reproach and self-castigation were behind me, and I had only a little way to go. The slope here was steep and I had to concentrate on walking, although soon it would be easy: I could already see the steps which led to the top. Here and there was a small wooden handrail, put there long ago to help the frail to climb to the wondrous view from the top.

I heard a train: far off at first but swiftly becoming louder. My heart gave a wild leap, and I missed a step. The train drew nearer, very fast; first its beating sound came, soon superseded by a hiss and a roar. I was within sight of it, not more than fifty yards away. It was coming from the west country, towards me. I could not see the wheels, only the bullet-shaped front of the locomotive. There was no smoke, no steam, no fire, only the ravenous roar and the thunder of the wheels on the rails, thunder and weight which shook the ground I stood on. The wind tore at me, like pointed claws.

The engine passed. I saw two men, halfway along it.

The coaches came, one after another, with people at the windows, faces streaked because of the distance and the train's speed, so that I could hardly tell which were men and which were women and which were boys and girls.

T'rump-t'rump—

It passed; it was gone.

Noise came back but was less fearsome. Instead of looking at the hurtling engine and the racing carriages there was only the blue sky beyond. Empty blueness.

I was without breath, the wind had been so fierce.

I stood still, clutching my hair.

I knew, now, what it would be like; what would happen if the monster had struck me; it would have been like a man crushing an insect.

One crushing, shattering impact: and I would be nothing.

Not even — *pieces.*

Nothing but — blood. Crushed bone and flesh. Blood. Shapeless; worse than shapeless, something which would never have shape again. Obliterated.

Easy, I had thought. *Easy!*

I had not moved since the train had passed, but now I was aware of the sounds of my own breathing; of the wind stirring my hair; of birds, flying here. And the sky. And in my ears was the screeching roar and in my head the thumping such as I had never known before.

Could — I — throw — myself — in — front — of — a — train?

Could I? Now.

If I did not, what would I do?

Go back to the house. Prepare an evening meal. Wait. Wait for Marcus and what he might do and what he might say. I could see his face. I could hear his voice. It was as loud as the roar of the train. If I went back what chance would I ever have of escape? What other way than death was there to break the invisible bonds which tied me to him?

I could not go back; I would do anything.

I heard a train, in the distance.

It was coming, like the other, from the west country. It was far off, like the other, but there was no mistaking its approach. Soon, it would be here. It would be here almost — not quite but almost — as soon as I reached the top, the line. Even now I would have to hurry. Hurry, hurry, hurry, hurry. It was coming. My fate was coming, all the darkness that had no shadow. Soon I would be nothing. If I hurried it could take me. Hurry, hurry, wait no longer. In my breast the call was like a tune, a siren's song. Hurry, hurry, *t'rump-t'rump*. Hurry, hurry, here I come. Hurry-hurry.

I began to run as best I could up the steep sides of the embankment. Now I could see the bullet front, the might of the monster, now the *t'rumping* was a roaring. Hurry, hurry!

I reached the level ground at the top of the hill. I had only to run, to climb the fence, to throw myself into the roar until it swallowed me up, obliterated me and took away all pain.

I'm coming, I almost screamed: I'm coming!

Then, as I began to run, a hand fell on my shoulder and another on my waist.

9

Fury

THERE WAS A HAND ON MY SHOULDER, AND A HAND ON MY waist. That was how Marcus gripped me whenever he was in a rage and when he was going to force me into obedience.

Marcus!

He must have followed —

The train was passing, roaring, the wind was clawing, and all the noise and all the fury seemed to bury itself within me, and then force itself out. I flung the hands off and turned around and clenched my fists and struck and struck and kicked and kicked at the man who had held me back, kept me from that longed-for oblivion.

It was not Marcus, but that did not matter.

His face, his body, was a blur. I could not hear anything he said. I kicked and punched and clawed at him, and I know also that I screamed; but I do not know what I screamed, except that two words seemed to be the fountain for them all. Hate— kill: hate — kill: hate — kill. The roaring from the engine and the train began to fade but the roaring in me did not; but now I was aware of other sounds without first knowing what they were. Gradually I became aware of them: the barking of a dog.

As gradually, I began to see; and to hear more clearly; and to understand.

This was the man whom I had seen down in the park. George Jees. He was snatching at the Dalmatian's leash as it tried to get at me, now barking, now snarling, now growling. With his other hand the man was trying to fend me off, pushing, not striking. Afterwards I realised that he would probably have turned and backed off but for the dog; had he allowed the dog its freedom then it would have done to me what I was trying to do to its master.

At last, I stopped.

I was gasping for breath, and each inward as well as each outward breath seemed to burn in my throat and to burn my lungs. I was standing but every muscle in my body was a-quiver and at any moment I would fall. The air would not go deep enough into my lungs, there were moments when it seemed that I could not draw sufficient in, that I would choke to death.

The man said: "Bend — forward. Slowly."

Bend — forward? Why, I thought. I gulped, and retched.

"It will help," he said, and then he turned to the dog and said sternly: "Sit, Spots, sit!" The dog was standing, straining at the leash and growling, but when the man allowed the leash to fall, he sat; or half-sat. "Now," the man said, "let me push you forward from the neck. It *will* help." I felt strong hands and firm but not harsh pressure at the back of my neck, and allowed myself to go forward. "Now back," he said. "Slowly — slowly. Forward again. Slowly — slowly." After he had spoken the rhythm a few times he stopped speaking and gasped for breath himself, until after a while breathing came more easily to me and I no longer had the feeling that my lungs would burst.

I managed to say: "I'm — all right."

He let me go, and the dog growled —and then sprang to its feet and for an instant I thought it would leap at me. But he was looking in another direction, downhill, and its tail was waving, its whole body was at tension. Into the new-found quiet came a cry.

"Come on, Spots! Spots!"

"Off you go," the man said, and on the 'go' the Dalmatian leapt down the hill towards the woman Jees who had appeared from a copse down in the park.

By that time I was breathing much more freely although still with an effort, and my legs were wobbly.

"I should sit down," the man advised in a conversational voice and added: "May I help you?" He took my hands and smiled pleasantly. "Just let yourself go. I won't let you fall."

I did what he said; and when I was sitting on the long, dry grass, tremors ran up my legs and through my body, but they were from the release of tension, not pain.

"Why don't you lie down?" he asked. "You'll feel even better."

"I — I'm all right."

"Sure," he said. "Sure. You're fine." He had a very good set of white teeth, and a strong face; and looked older than I had thought. He moved a few paces away and dropped to the ground, squatting cross-legged without effort. "Esmé will be here in a few minutes. I'm George."

"George — Jees. I know."

"So you did hear what she said when you met."

"Of course," I replied.

"Sorry, sorry," he said hastily — placatingly. "She didn't think you took very much in." His eyes crinkled at the corners as he smiled.

For the first time I noticed a scratch on his cheek, at one side near the ear; blood was oozing from this and beginning to trickle down his neck. There were some slight weals, too, the marks of nails: my nails as I had attacked him. He saw where I was looking and touched the scratch;

the ball of his forefinger crimsoned. His eyes rounded, he dried the finger on the grass and then took out a crumpled handkerchief, folded it, and dabbed the scratch.

"Is that my only wound?" he asked lightly.

"As far as I can see," I told him.

"You deserved to cause better scars," he said.

I gave an involuntary little shudder.

"Please don't!"

"No, ma'am," he said, with a comical raising of his fair eyebrows. "On the other hand now — I'm not so sure."

"Not — not so sure of what?"

"That while the facts are hot in your mind and the evidence clear on my face, that you shouldn't look at those facts."

"I — I don't want to think of it!"

"How long have you been doing this?" he asked.

"Doing what?"

"Contemplating such drastic action."

"That is — insulting."

"Oh, sure," he agreed lightly. "The truth often is. But it remains the truth. Did you realise that was the ultimate in escapism?"

I began to feel genuine resentment and my voice sharpened: "What is?"

"Suicide."

I remember that as I looked at him his expression changed and the light in his blue eyes hardened, his lips set. Was that a reflection of the way I was looking? For the first time since I had been able to breathe freely I was beginning to feel and to realise what had happened. I would have thrown myself in front of that train; but for this man all the pain and fears and anguish would be gone.

I said: "I wanted to die. I have a right to kill myself. I shall kill myself. You've simply wasted your time."

For some seconds he looked at me without a change

of expression; and I had no idea what he was going to say. I only know that at the time I meant exactly what I said and that resentment was building up in me against this man who had pulled me back from the oblivion I had wanted.

Suddenly, totally unexpectedly, he grinned; and his eyes and his whole face lit up, as if with sheer enjoyment. There was a chuckle in his voice as he said:

"Well, it was a good try, and you may not pluck up courage to try again. I hope you won't. You're far too pretty and young to die."

10

Hiding Place

I SIMPLY COULD NOT ANSWER HIM. I REMEMBER BEGINNING to say: "So you admit it takes courage," but the words would not come, and I looked away from him. The Dalmatian came rushing up, circled George Jees and raced to his wife who was only a hundred yards or so away. Up here with the full sunlight upon it, her hair looked more copper-coloured than red; I had never seen a lovelier colour in a woman's hair. The coppery look was in her skin, too, and her eyes, also catching the sun, were more honey-brown than green-flecked brown.

She, too, was smiling.

The dog, now having a game of racing from one to the other, looked as if he were grinning.

They were the nearest I could imagine to a happy trio.

At last, Esmé Jees came up, and flopped on to the ground.

"That's a steeper hill than it looks," she remarked.

"Spots makes light of it," her husband observed.

"He's all muscle and bone and no sense." Esmé was looking at the side of his face; the scratch. But she made no comment on that as she turned to me, and, still smiling and yet quite out of the blue, went on: "Please don't hate us."

"She does," George declared.

"Be quiet, honey. *Please* don't," Esmé Jees repeated, earnestly. "You will be glad. I'm sure you will."

I did not respond.

"We have been discussing the wisdom of facing facts now," George told her. "I advised yes, on the whole — they fade so soon. A fact is not a fact when it happened yesterday."

"Must you make jokes, honey?"

"That was not a joke. It was a remark born of deep philosophical conviction."

"That must be why it wasn't funny," Esmé said. "What have you been saying to her?"

"I asked her how long she had been running away from herself. And facts. I also said that suicide was the ultimate escapism."

"Escape," Esmé corrected.

"We don't know," said George. "What if there is a state of purgatory and we have to relive all we've done in this life?"

"George — "

"Honey, you wouldn't be helping our pretty neighbour to run away from facts, would you? After all, I was but the tool of your conviction, the method you used to bring her back from the brink." All this time he was watching me closely and I needed no telling that he was testing me: I suspected, hoping that he could spur me into talking while being afraid that once we went down to the park and reached our homes I would not talk at all. "Wonder what I mean by that?" he asked me, and when I didn't reply he went on in the same half-jocular, half-serious way: "When she came to visit you three weeks ago, Esmé thought you were in a state of very high tension. And we've both wondered if you have problems and have been watching you. Nosey Parkers, you might say. I came the back way to the park," he added, "to make sure you couldn't guess that you were being followed."

At last, he stopped.

Esmé raised her hands and let them fall, rather help-lessly. I turned to look down into the park and the houses — and on that instant a train sounded in the distance and the earth beneath us quivered, very slightly at first and then more violently. The *t'rump-t'rump* became very loud, and the roar was so great and the wind so fierce that involuntarily all three of us turned our heads away.

Soon, it passed.

"I don't think we should stay here," Esmé said.

"Sweet thing," said George, "you *are* encouraging her to turn away from facts."

"Honey, you're being cruel."

"Sometimes one has to be cruel to be kind."

One trite, trite remark: worthy of Marcus in full flood.

"George — "

"Esmé, my pet, ten minutes or so ago I drew this young woman back from an ugly death. She owes me something. I don't think a 'there, there, dear, dear, don't worry, honey' will do her any good at all. Janetta" — now he was wholly serious and looked at me with rare intensity as he went on — "why did you try to kill yourself? What guilty secret goads you? What makes you feel life's not worth living? What or who are you afraid of? Life?" He paused, but was already forming another word and it came very deliberately: "Your husband?" Another pause and this time he raised his hand and pointed a steady forefinger at me: "Or yourself?"

For what seemed a long time there was silence.

Esmé broke it with an anguished: "George!"

Out of myself, almost unbidden, came an answer which I can hear whenever I think back to that dreadful afternoon; it did not seem to be my voice, it was so husky and so hollow.

"All three," I said. "All three."

Next moment I hated myself, for I began to cry.

Between them, they helped me down. Parked on a path where it should not have been was the little red Fiat, and they helped me into the seat next to the driver's and then George took the wheel and Esmé called the dog who had gone hunting. George did not talk as he drove, steadily, to the road which skirted Dingle Park and then along the bisecting thoroughfare which had turnings off on either side, each turning leading to a network of narrow streets, past the square houses which were like dolls' houses in their pretty colours. He drew into the kerb, said: "Stay here," and jumped out and opened the double gates — once, there had been a garage just inside the garden.

As the gates clanged, he was back at the wheel.

"I'll drive it," he said. "You won't feel like a peep show." He manoeuvred the little car as if it were a bicycle, and backed in; when he opened the door for me I stepped out almost on to the tiny porch.

Tears were still streaming down my cheeks, I was utterly out of control: helpless. He put an arm round my waist and half pushed me on to the porch; I stumbled on to the front step. He turned his key in the front door lock and pushed me into the hall which was at once identical and yet so different from my house. He kicked open the door of the front room, which was filled with bamboo furniture and scrolls and colourful paintings and a raffia mat. One wall was filled with these pictures, but I did not see that until later; I saw only the bamboo bed or chaise-longue alongside it, with brightly-coloured cushions.

"On you get," he said. "I'll go and make some coffee."

He left me alone for the first time since his hand had

fallen on my shoulder. I was still crying. I stretched out, on my side; then turned face downwards, biting into one of the cushions. I have no idea how long I was like that, alone; I was vaguely aware of sounds and voice but they meant nothing to me for a long time.

Slowly, I came out of the paroxysm.

Now and again I gave a combination of a sigh and a gargantuan sob, but no tears came and even the misery was less.

The time came when I eased myself on to one side again and punched the cushion for greater comfort. I was beginning to think and even to wonder where the others were and how long they would be. I became aware, too, of the familiar sounds; and then one which was unfamiliar, the sniffing of a dog outside the door.

"Spots — come away." That was Esmé, in a whisper.

"Spots — sit."

I could imagine how he sat, forelegs wide apart, mouth open, eyes turned towards his mistress.

"Don't move."

There was a creak at the door, and Esmé appeared, just her burnished head and face at first, then her shoulders. She peered towards me, and could see my face for George had put me with my head towards the window.

"I'm all right," I managed to say.

She came in quickly, quietly.

"Why, you look much better!"

"I must look terrible."

"You look repairable," she said, and her eyes seemed to dance. "*Really* feel better?"

"Yes," I said. "Much."

"Like some coffee?"

"I would love some."

"George has it perking," she said, and turned towards

the passage, but she didn't go out of the room. "Ready, George."

"Coming!" called her husband, while she came right into the room and I began to struggle up. "The back of that chaise rises," she said, "just sit upright." Ratchets rasped, I felt the upright section firm against my back, and she punched and pushed a pillow in position. "Would you like to loosen your skirt?" she asked.

"No, I'm comfortable — I really am."

And I was. My shoes were on the floor, George must have pulled them off, and my feet were a little chilly, that was all. Esmé pulled up a bamboo stool, and kicked another into position as George came in bearing a wooden tray with a tall percolator and wide-brimmed cups, sugar, and some biscuits — plain and cream and chocolate-covered. He placed this on a corner of the chaise I was on, and asked:

"Cream and sugar?"

"White, please," I said. "And a little sugar."

"A lot of sugar. It's good for shock. Cookies?" He handed the plate of biscuits to Esmé who held them out to me.

I took a chocolate-covered wafer biscuit; drank two cups of coffee; took two more of the 'cookies'; watched them eating and drinking with obvious relish. There was no doubt at all, they did seem happy, there was a quality of gaiety in them; and more, a quality which made me feel as if I had known them for years.

Suddenly, I asked: "Who plays the piano?"

"We both do," Esmé said.

"Chopin's *Prelude in C Minor*."

"Esmé," declared George, emphatically. "She's the classicist."

"Do you play?" Esmé asked.

"I used to."

"Why don't you now?"

"I've no piano."

"But surely —" Esmé began, only to break off short.

"In this day and age a piano isn't so costly that you can't get one," George said.

"It's not —" I began, and broke off in turn. Then: "My husband doesn't like to hear me playing."

"Good God!" exclaimed George.

"For land's sakes," said Esmé. "What is he, tone-deaf or something?"

"He — he doesn't like it because —"

I hesitated, with the words bubbling up within me and my mind telling me not to talk, to keep all these things bottled up. Perhaps had either of them tried to persuade me to talk at that moment I would have simply shut the truth away; but neither made any attempt to urge me, and the story that was hidden deep in me pushed itself to the surface.

"He hates it because I used to play to my first husband."

"Gosh!" exclaimed Esmé.

"A jealous man is a jealous man," George declared with that pretended earnestness; he knew how cliché-ridden his talk could be: it was deliberate, a way of making me think more about him than about what I was saying.

"What happened to your first husband?" asked Esmé.

"Unintelligent question," George put in. "Divorced, of course."

"For —" Esmé began, and then added in a higher-pitched voice: "It's no business of ours."

"Never did you say a truer word," declared George.

"Honey, this isn't —"

"Funny. I know."

"Was murdered," I said, in a scarcely audible voice.

"What?" asked George.

"*Murd*ered!" echoed Esmé, as if she would choke.

"Don't be a ghoul," George protested.

"George — "

"He *was* murdered."

"Jehosophat!" gasped Esmé, helplessly.

"You did say — " began George, and then he pushed his stool back. "My heavens. Janetta, I'm — I'm sorry."

"It — it's all right."

"I didn't hear what you said before."

"It's all right, really."

"Murdered," Esmé said, and, swallowing the word, asked: "How?"

"Poisoned."

"Who — " Esmé began, and stopped as if someone had chopped the words away from her lips.

"Was the murderer found?" asked George.

"Yes — yes. I suppose so."

"You suppose so!" Esmé's voice had never been so sharp.

"He — he was in love with another woman. She — she was found guilty."

"His mistress," George said in a muffled voice. "What a — what an incredible story." His eyes seemed to be boring into me. "Did you know her?"

"No," I answered, gasping. "No! I never met her."

"What — what is it like to know that your husband has a mistress?" asked Esmé in a wondering voice. "To know that he would rather sleep with — "

"Honey," George interrupted, "you put too much emphasis on whom a man sleeps with. It's a modern, post-Victorian phenomenon — this concern is, I mean."

"Doesn't it make you *hate* him?" asked Esmé and she was looking at me quite as intently as George. "Doesn't it make you want — "

"Enough!" cried George.

"George, I — "

"Do you mean your second husband knowing that you used to make music for your first husband, decided that music — piano music — was out? He is such a — flint-heart?" George demanded. "Great heavenly hosts."

"But how did you feel?" demanded Esmé. "How long did you know that he had a mistress? Oh, it must have been dreadful!"

"Some wives feel that it removes some of the responsibility from them," put in George. "Remember Victor Hugo. 'This is the wife of my kitchen . . . this is the wife of my bed.' And the two spouses did not appear to hit each other over the heads with skillets and bed-warmers."

This time, Esmé did not protest, and although I heard what George said I was not thinking of the words or their meaning.

I was thinking that I had lied to the police about not knowing that Anthony had a mistress. That through all the questioning I had stuck to that because I was sure that if I had admitted knowing, then I would be a suspect and I might be put on trial.

At that time I had been sure that I had not killed Anthony. But could I now be sure? Was the desire to kill inherent in me? Frustrated, angered, embittered, had I not wished Anthony dead; as now, frustrated, angered and embittered but for different reasons, did I not long — *long* — to kill Marcus?

George was standing and looking down on me; Esmé was sitting and looking straight at me; and in their gaze was a great intensity. It was as if they were willing me to tell the truth, all the truth of the things which went on in my mind and had driven me to the day's extremity.

Suddenly, George said: "Why did you try to kill yourself, Janetta? I asked you before and I'll ask you again. And until you have seen the truth and faced it you will never be able to live with yourself. Was it because of yourself? Or your husband? Or simply weariness with life?"

There was silence until Esmé whispered:

"Why, Janetta? Why?"

As I looked from one to the other, aware of their great intensity, it was as if they had brought me here so that they could ask these questions and make me talk.

Then, I remembered: she had not really come to me that day for a cupful of sugar. And I remembered that they had watched and followed me. Now above all other things I wanted to find out *why*.

11

Why?

"JANETTA," ESMÉ SAID, "WHY DID YOU TRY TO KILL YOURSELF?"

"Janetta," said George, gently and yet with a steely voice, "why can't you live with yourself?"

Inwardly I asked them both: Why are you here? Why are you asking me all these questions?

"When you've faced the truth you will be able to live with it," George went on.

"It's no use lying to yourself," Esmé said in an unsteady voice. "Janetta—"

I asked very quietly: "Who are you two?"

The question startled them, George I thought more than Esmé but both were taken aback and they exchanged swift glances, secret glances, before they looked back at me.

"I told you — " Esmé began.

"You nearly broke the front door down to make me answer. Was that really for some sugar?"

She was taken aback even more; and sat back. Outside the dog whined and the sound seemed very loud.

"Janetta — " George began.

"Why were you watching me?" I demanded, and then with a vehemence which even surprised me, I went on: "Why didn't you want me to die? Why were you watching? Why had you brought the car so close? Why did you smuggle me in here?" Now that the questions had begun they poured out, some from the surface and some from the depth of my mind. "Who are you?" I cried. "What are you doing to me? How do you know my name so well? Tell me — who *are* you? What are you doing to me?"

They sat silent. In a way it was a guilty silence; or at least a helpless one. They exchanged glances again, and George gave an expressive shrug of his shoulders. I had demanded to know who they were and yet in a way I seemed to know them well, better than anyone I had known since — since Anthony.

The dog was sniffing and beginning to whine again.

"For heaven's sake!" I exclaimed. "Why don't you let that animal in?"

"Ah," said George, in a flat voice. "Yes. He is excited because you — ah — we got excited. All right, Spots," he said, and turned and opened the door. The dog took one comprehensive look at its master and mistress and a scornful one at me, and leapt up at George, paws almost reaching his shoulders, tongue seeking his chin or his face. George played with the floppy ears for a moment and then said: "Down, Spots." The dog immediately dropped to all fours. "Isn't Spots a ridiculous name for a Dalmatian?" he asked. "Sit, Spots."

"When I was young," I said, "I knew Dalmatian twins. One was Plum and the other was Duff."

"I don't understand," said Esmé, with a puzzled glance at her husband, who gave a rueful laugh and replied:

"That shows how un-English you are. Plum Duff: one name for a suet pudding dotted with black currants or sultanas."

"Seedless raisins?"

"I have called them that."

"Currants," I insisted, absurdly.

"Sometimes called Spotted Dick," he observed. "Even Spotted *Dog!*"

"I give up," said Esmé, looking defeated.

"You're *English*!" I accused George Jees.

"I cannot tell a lie," he said.

"Stop playing the fool!" protested Esmé.

"Yes," I agreed. "Yes. Stop playing the fool. *Are* you English?"

"I've lived in America for over twenty-five years," George said. "Some of my school and all my college days. And I've nearly lost the British accent. Yes. I am English." He began to speak very solemnly. "My family is English, too."

"Family," I said.

"Yes. You really *have* no idea, have you?" said George; he sounded as if he were marvelling. "None at all."

"About what?" I cried.

"His family," Esmé answered for him. "Two brothers and a sister."

"What on earth has that got to do with me?" I demanded. I was vexed in one way, puzzled and curious in another. They had started to play some game with me and I had no idea what it was — could not even begin to think. I knew it was significant; I had no doubt at all that they had answers to all my questions, answers which could appal me. "*Please —* " I stretched out my hands to George. "Tell me."

George looked down on me. Then with great precision he said: "Oh, hell." Then he took my hands; his were cold and, as I already knew, very powerful. "I shall have to tell her," he said to Esmé while looking at me. His eyes, so blue outside, had the greyness of ice in here. "My sister's name is Hilary," he stated simply.

"Hilary," I echoed.

Hilary, I thought.

"Hilary!" I cried, and gripped his hands as if mine were claws. "Anthony's — mistress! Her."

"That's right," George confirmed, quietly. "My only sister." He looked so stern, so like a judge; he held my fingers tightly and yet there was not simply friendliness and succour in his eyes: there was accusation. "Lingering in prison," he went on. "For killing your husband. I wish to God you were not what you seem to be."

Slowly, very slowly, my fingers slid from George's grasp. As slowly I leaned back on the chaise-longue, as if something was urging me to get as far away from him as I could. He did not change his expression or look away from me, and something of the bitterness in those last words showed in the set of his lips and in his eyes.

Spots growled: a low-pitched sound. Esmé stretched out her hand, and, as he moved towards her, put the hand on his head, to soothe him. He sat down, front feet in front of him, rear legs folded beneath him: a Dalmatian couchant.

I had only seen Hilary in the dock.

I had not been in the witness stand for long; long enough only to be asked if I knew her and if I knew of my late husband's association with her. Two answers sufficed: "No." "No." I had seen her pictures in the newspapers. She had been a dark-haired woman with an olive complexion; beautiful in a Southern European way but not at all like this grey-blue eyed man who stood so lean and spare, looking at me searchingly.

I made myself ask: "What are you doing here?"

George raised his hands and placed the heels against his temples, and answered without looking away from me:

"To put you where Hilary is."

I said: "To — put — " and then I stopped, although I knew full well what he meant: he had come because he had believed that I had killed Anthony and had allowed his sister to take the blame. *That was what he believed.* It touched me with horror, the greater because if he asked me I could not absolutely swear that I had not.

And he would ask me.

There were so many other things I wanted to ask, so much that needed explanation, and yet the inevitable question was the only one that mattered. And as I waited for it, I felt a kind of relief; calm. I would not have to run away any more. I would not, no matter what the temptation. Whatever he asked me, I would tell the truth as far as I knew it.

"Janetta," he said, "did you kill Anthony?"

Slowly, heavily, I replied: "I don't — don't know."

He flashed: "You must know!"

"I don't know," I insisted. "I don't — believe so, but I am sometimes terrified in case I did."

"You know," he said, in a strained voice, "you are not making much sense."

"No," I agreed, and from somewhere found a high-pitched laugh. "I haven't been making much sense to myself for a long time. I — I sometimes felt that I could kill him."

"For taking another woman?"

"Yes."

"Did you know, before his death?" Now his eyes were ice-cold again, as if he were forcing back anger; as if he were fighting to keep calm and wanted to rave at me.

I said, haltingly: "That is the one thing I know I lied about. Yes, I knew there was another woman."

"Did you know who she was?"

"No, I did not. Just the name, Hilary."

"Janetta, tell the whole truth." The bristling in his tone accused me of lying, he was more aggressive than he had yet been; even his body tensed and his hands clenched. "Understand — tell the whole truth."

Wearily, I replied: "I can't because I don't know the whole truth. There were times when I hated what he was doing to me so much that I felt that I could kill him, although" — now I spread my hands towards him appealingly — "I had forgotten that. Completely forgotten, until — until I began to hate Marcus: to long to kill *him*. It seemed the only way to escape, the only way out of misery, and — and then I began to wonder. *Did* I kill Anthony? Is — is killing inherent in me? Is it?" I did not move my hands, they were extended now in supplication, the same supplication that was in my voice. "I — I know one thing. I would kill Marcus if the only alternative was to go on living with him. That is why I preferred to kill myself."

I stopped, and slowly withdrew my hands. I realised that Esmé was with us; for what seemed an age I had forgotten her as well as the dog, who was quiet now except for quick, panting breath.

I had told the truth: there was no way of proving it, but what I had told them was the truth as I knew it — that I might have killed Anthony: that I would kill Marcus rather than go on living with him: that there were gaps in my memory which I could not explain. The silence which followed went on and on; and at first it seemed to me a damning silence. How could I reasonably expect them to believe me? How —

"You know," George said quietly, "it's so crazy it's almost convincing. Janetta, let me tell you something now. I could not believe Hilary had killed Anthony. It made no sense to me. There was no reason why she should, her husband knew about her *affaire* and was staying with her because of the children. It wasn't a happy household but Ben's a remarkable man and Hilary is a remarkable woman, and they made it bearable.

"I came over for the trial, but Esmé was having health problems, the doctors thought it was terminal cancer. So I had to go back. It was cancer but it yielded to surgery, and as soon as we were sure we came to England, buying a houseful of furniture at an auction sale. We did a great deal of checking around before finally we came here to check on you. I was bloody nearly sure that you were the murderer and we came here ready to hate you. But — "

Into his pause, Esmé said: "We couldn't; we just could not make ourselves."

"Although it looked as if you had a heavy load on your conscience," said George. "We thought — we still think — you killed him but we'll never prove it by the ordinary processes of the law." With a quick aside, more like his usual self, he asked Esmé: "How'm I doing?"

She did not answer.

"So, will you help us to find the truth?" George demanded; his voice lost its vigour and was almost shrill.

"Help you prove *I* killed Anthony?" I could only gasp out the words and gape at him.

"If that is the truth, yes," he said, his voice still tinny. "The one question is: did you or didn't you? *You* really want to know, don't you?" When I didn't answer immediately he went on more roughly: "Or do you simply want soothing syrup: the truth if it lets you off the hook, but the same old half-truths and wool-over-the-eyes amnesia if it would put you where Hilary is?"

Effortfully, I answered: "I want the truth. I want to know the truth whatever it costs me. But — " I raised my hands towards him again; it was almost pathetic, how I had come to need his help. "But how can I find out? How can *you* find out?"

"We know a man who probably can," George said.

"We know he can!" exclaimed Esmé, excitedly.

"We think he can," said George, soberly. "We consulted

him about Hilary before and after the trial, he was said to
be the one man who could dig the truth out of any human
being, no matter how many overlays of lies and self-deceit
there were. He is more than a psychiatrist, he is — well,
Esmé thinks he is the wisest man she has ever known."
After a pause, George moved forward and took my hands
and gripped them so tightly that it hurt: now *he* was
pleading; and Esmé was, too, with her eyes, with her whole
being. "He is a man named Cellini, Doctor Emmanuel
Cellini, and he's great — I swear to you he's great. Will
you see him? Let him talk to you and do what he asks
you to. Will you? All he will look for in you is the truth."

George stood over me — pleading.

Esmé leaned forward and looked at me — pleading.

I had a sense that they wanted only the truth. There was
no way of being sure, but the feeling was so strong that
it overcame all the doubts and hesitations. There was
more: that deep, compulsive need to know with certainty
whether I had killed Anthony.

If this man — Cellini? Was it Cellini? — could help to
find it then I simply had to see him.

"Yes," I answered, very quietly. "And I would like to
see him soon."

"I talked to him this morning," George said, quickly.
"He may be free to come this evening, certainly tomorrow.
Meanwhile — " He backed away from me and then looked
down on me worriedly. "What will you do meanwhile?
Will you stay here with us? Or go back to Marcus?"

"I shall go back," I decided. "I shall be all right for one
night, I'm sure." I hardly knew what prompted me to add
with wry humour: "He'll be quite safe."

It was good to hear their laughter, and to see the
Dalmatian frolic, happy because they were happy.

I almost felt that I was, too.

Dread of spending the night with Marcus was over-shadowed by the strange hope of seeing Dr. Cellini, 'the wisest man Esmé had ever known'.

Even the fear of what he might discover was dulled in an excitement, a euphoria, so strong that it was almost frightening in itself.

BOOK II

DR. CELLINI

12

I am Dr. Emmanuel Cellini

THERE IS NO DOUBT THAT TO SOME PEOPLE, ESPECIALLY young people, I am old; perhaps very old. And I confess that there are times when I am so physically weary that my bones and flesh seem old and weary and I feel that I cannot go on. Also, there are times when I am so disheartened and dispirited by what I see in human nature, the folly of human kind or the cruelty of society where it squeezes hope out of the individual who, at one time, lived and thrived on hope and faith in the future.

My wife, Felisa, scolds and scoffs when I talk of being old.

"Tired, Manny, tired — that is all. You are so young you make even young people old. What is it you say when you are talking to others? One is as old as one feels, yes — and most of the time, do you feel old?"

"Not truly old," I answer her. "Not all the time."

At times she will thrust a mirror in front of me and say: "Look good at yourself, ancient one! Does your white hair make you old — the silver of its colour belongs to all ages. And because you love those long moustaches you hide your mouth and your strong teeth — all your own — admit that is so, ancient one!" And she will press her face close to mine and point at our reflections. "Now, is not your skin as good as mine and free from all blemish

—with just soap and water! How many would envy you the baby's skin. Old! Never let me hear you say that again."

At times she can even make me puff out my chest with pride, for I have been fortunate, and my body absorbs the food I like without making me fat; not even plump. I will secretly glance at myself and think of the young man in his strength climbing his native Italian alps and I think I do not look so very different now. And for thirty years the same dinner suit has fitted me at the waist. I am not tall, no; when I was young I bemoaned my lack of inches. But the years compensate. "What use is height?" I now say, "except to see over the heads of others in a crowd, when one should be at the front, not at the back!"

But often a day in the Assize Court, or a day with a particularly complex human being upon whom I shall have to pronounce judgment — professional, not legal judgment — will make me very tired.

"You work too hard," Felisa will then scold. "In the days when we met you were working day and night to help people to escape from Germany, and afterwards from Austria." (That is how we met, Felisa and I, in an Austrian mountain village where I came for food.) "Why, you worked so hard you almost forgot to escape from Mussolini yourself!"

I will smile and tease, knowing what she wants.

"If my memory serves I almost forgot to save you."

"*Ja*, wicked one — so anxious were you to help those other young women that the woman who was to be your wife, Felisa, she did not matter."

"To this day," I tell her, "I wonder if I would have come back for you, had you not been such a good cook."

And that is always the time we stop the badinage, and remember the camps and the fear and the thump of feet and the thudding on the doors; the disappearance of our friends, the horor of a world which was replacing the one which, despite its many faults, Felisa and I loved so much.

It is not often that we brood over the past.

In some ways my life and hers really began when we arrived, with little but our clothes and a few trinkets and personal possessions, in London. We were not the only refugees! There was a register of people who would help such as us: some were refugees who had brought an amplitude with them, or had placed money in English or American banks; some were English, or Americans living in London, who were prepared, for a while at least, to help the nearly destitute.

We fell among friends; a doctor who had heard of my experiments in Italy and Austria, and was curious: and his wife. From this there sprang a long friendship, and they are happy to this day, living in a cottage not far from London, and whenever Felisa and I go there for a week-end, Felisa does the cooking. Two phrases are inevitable, during that meal, which is always eaten by the light of candles which glow on the red of the wine in the tall-stemmed glasses, or the pale amber; and which are reflected in the polished surface of a refectory table once used by monks in a nearby abbey — ruined, now, a legacy of Cromwell — and waxed and polished over the centuries.

"If it weren't for Felisa," my doctor friend would say, "Agnes would never be able to cook a meal."

For Felisa was a good teacher of cooking, especially dishes such as apple strudel and omelettes, veal cooked in wine, even the famed Sacher cake.

And, a little later: "If you hadn't been filled with silly notions of a new method of psychiatry, of worshipping at the feet of a new Freud, you would never have become the second most eminent psychiatrist in England," Agnes would say.

"Shall I ever forget it?" my friend would agree. "I thought he had a new method, almost a mystique, and all he had was applied common sense. Manny, sometimes I think you are still an old fraud. *Did* you ever study psychology and — "

That was when Felisa and Agnes would leave us, to talk.

Usually, Felisa would be asleep, in the huge four-poster bed which left hardly room to move about, when I crept up the wooden stairs, three centuries old, and then slipped quietly under the feather quilt.

It is true that I am not a conventional psychiatrist. I have of course to accept something of both the teachings of Freud and Jung, even agree with some of their disciples who — like Christ's — attributed to their masters much which their masters did not say or teach. I had long since learned that the first essential quality of a psychiatrist was the ability to listen without allowing one's attention to wander. Those who are in great mental stress and emotional turmoil are for the most part highly sensitive. They begin to talk with great caution, even reluctance, then begin to feel at ease. If their confidant's attention wanders, by the lifting of an eye towards a door; by a sigh; by any interruption badly timed, then the confidence so slowly and painstakingly established can be broken; often, it cannot properly be repaired.

Some are by nature listeners; some talkers; I, by some grace I do not understand, am both, each complementing the other. I have learned not to allow them to overlap at the wrong time.

The first essential, then, is to be able to listen.

The second, is to be able to understand the immense burden that a trifle can place on the mind of a man or woman. It is too often said that it is the last straw which breaks a camel's back. The truth is that the camel's burden is made of single straws and the cumulative weight does the breaking. The human's burden is made up of a mass of trifles, each with its own special significance, its capacity to cause fear, grief, pain, anxiety far greater at some moments and in some moods than at others.

What the doctor must find — what *I* must find — is what is causing the consciousness of burden at a given time. What is oppressing the mind? To find this is never easy and usually takes a great deal of time, for generally speaking only those in the extremity of a psychotic or neurotic illness are brought to me for treatment. Too often, it is too late.

Two things one learns without realising that the layman seldom fully understands them. First, that outwardly a patient can be absolutely normal, or appear to be normal, most of the time. I can never understand why this puzzles so many people. After all, countless thousands with cancer, or heart disease, or some sickness of the blood, can and do appear normal up to the moment of final collapse.

"He looked so *well*."

"Whoever would have thought *he* was ill?"

"You never know, do you?"

The mind, of course, can secrete symptoms of sickness more cleverly than the body. Madness can work in the most unsuspected places; and indeed does. Ninety-nine times out of a hundred it is a harmless madness, but the hundredth time it can be deadly.

Physical pain and sickness can be relieved and the cause often diagnosed; but mental pain and anguish, often more serious than the physical, are seldom really relieved by drugs and tranquillisers or alcohol. The misery remains; and I have come. in my sixty-and-more years, to believe that the world's greatest sickness is human misery.

When it is visible, as famine, pestilence, thirst and brutality, it can be so easily diagnosed, and the cure is easy;

if the means to feed a starving man is at hand and he is forever afterwards fed well, he is rarely likely to suffer because he once was near death through starvation. But a sickness of the mind, once there, can — it does not always but it can — linger until it becomes incurable and sometimes deadly.

But once the cause is found, and removed, then the operation is far more likely to be a lifelong success than an operation for a malignant growth. The danger is that it is far more difficult to find, because it is often buried so deep, than any physical sickness. The diagnosis is inordinately complicated. It may not take long — or it may take weeks and months — but let none think it easy even at the most experienced hands.

For each mind is different.

The complexity of the human body is negligible compared with that of the human mind.

The complexity of the human mind is less, far less, than the emotional complexity of the human spirit.

And the nerve-tissues of the mind and spirit are of such delicacy that they can be tortured by a careless word; by the wrong diagnosis; by the wrong treatment. The second vital thing in my life's task then is to remember that each patient is different from all the others.

In some ways the most fascinating patient I have ever tried to help was a young woman named Janetta Hunter.

I first saw Janetta — her name then was Janetta Grey — in an Assize Court when another woman was on trial for the murder of Anthony Grey, Janetta's husband. I was an expert witness in the case, called to testify that in my opinion the accused was sane within the legal meaning of the word. In fact I did not find Hilary Consett a particularly interesting individual. She was a very pleasant, warm-hearted person, a good mother to her three children and a competent housewife. I suspected that she was considerably 'over-sexed' in the sense that she was not easily satisfied sexually and for her peace of mind — contentment of mind and body, in fact — needed more than the occasional attention her husband could give her, for he was away a great deal.

Hilary Consett formed an attachment with Anthony Grey, an accountant in the firm for which her husband worked. I do not know the details of how they met or what happened but I do know that he was able to satisfy her needs — and it later transpired, she his, to the neglect of his wife — and that this mutual satisfaction continued for a year or more until, one day, Anthony Grey was taken ill with severe sickness and stomach cramps, and died in hospital.

The cause was arsenic poisoning; the source of the arsenic, chocolates of a brand name *Alconut*. The chocolates, all of which contained nuts and raisins and were highly flavoured, had been treated with arsenic in a simple, easy to detect way. A small hole drilled or melted in each, an arsenic paste carefully inserted, the hole then sealed with melted chocolate — it was quite easy.

Hilary Consett was proved to be Grey's mistress; often bought *Alconut* chocolate bars, and used arsenic in a weed-killer frequently. She was charged with the murder, convicted, and sentenced to imprisonment for life, which in her case was likely to be ten to fifteen years.

She had denied her guilt from the beginning.

I had followed the case partly because I was being consulted, partly because of my friend Detective Superintendent John Hardy, of the Criminal Investigation Department at Scotland Yard. John Hardy was above all things, even above his profession, a humanitarian. He worried about some of his cases, and this one had got under his skin. Whenever this happened he would come and discuss it with me. A bachelor, he was by way of being a gourmet, and Felisa's cooking alone would have been enough of an attraction.

On the evening when he had talked to me about Hilary Consett, he said:

"She bought bars of chocolate regularly for Anthony Grey and herself — a little luxury indulgence for their evenings together. They didn't have much luxury, Manny. He bought an old caravan, and rented some space in a field a few miles away from their homes — they both live near Hendleton."

Hendleton is a big dormitory suburb about fifteen miles south-west of London; my side of London, although several miles away.

"And that was their love nest?" Felisa asked. On such an evening as this she liked to sit and listen.

"That's where they disported themselves," Hardly confirmed. "Ocasionally he bought a carton of the chocolates, which can only be obtained at the better shops. It's a high-priced brand, packed only in two sizes: small tablets and in flat half-pound boxes fitted with small squares. The boxes fit into a pocket. And although he told Hilary Consett he never took them home in fact an opened packet was found in a small writing desk in his home. He did some accountancy, mostly tax work, at home."

"Whenever did he find the time? My goodness!" exclaimed Felisa.

"He was always home at weekends and the assignations were seldom more than twice although sometimes three times a week," Hardy told her. "His wife, a much more interesting person than the accused, Manny, says she didn't know the chocolates were there."

"Do you believe her?"

"I think so," Hardy said, and his manner betrayed at least

a modicum of doubt. "She also swears she didn't know her husband was having an *affaire*."

"Nonsense, nonsense!" Felisa declared. "A woman of perception always knows."

"Likes to think she knows," I murmured, teasingly.

"Such a man, who thinks he is so clever!" Felisa rounded on me. She is a short woman, even shorter than I am, and full-bosomed, and she dresses in an old-fashioned way, loving the necklaces which cascade like a waterfall in front of her. Her favourite, perhaps, is amber, beautiful Polish amber; but she also loves the Tibetan agate, and the polished stones which friends in America send her, turquoise and silver shining and shimmering. She has a pale face, fine, strong features, dark eyes — and, whisper please, she has her hair touched up at every visit to the hairdresser so that it is not a mountain of white but of misty blue-grey. "Sometimes I wonder if John" — she pronounced his name with a soft 'sh' instead of a 'j'; a kind of 'zshon' sound which was most attractive — "comes here to get my opinion, not yours. Such nonsense. She said she did not know, John; then, she lies to you."

She was probably right, but not by any means for certain. Yet the more I heard of the case the more I thought that Janetta Grey did lie about that. Yet I was not sure. Once, John Hardy questioned her while I was in the other room, able to hear what was said, and when he asked for my opinion I had to tell him that I could not be sure.

Knowing about the long-standing *affaire*, Janetta Grey would have had a motive. Knowing about the chocolates, she would have had the weapon. Knowing about neither —

"What motive would Hilary Consett have?" I asked.

"At last, a good question," Felisa conceded; and patted my hand, mine so thin and veined and freckled, hers so plump and still so pink.

"Three," answered Hardy. "She may have wanted to

end the *affaire* and he have refused. She may have wanted him to divorce his wife, and he have refused. Or he might have wanted her to get a divorce and tried to force the issue, and she may have refused."

"Which one will you endeavour to prove in the prosecution?" I asked gently.

"I think I can establish that she wanted to end the *affaire* because she had found another lover," Hardy replied. "Alternatively, that Ben Consett was prepared for a full reconciliation but Anthony Grey refused to bow out. The facts are: she had the chocolates. She had arsenic — bought as a weed-killer and found in her toolshed. She had the opportunity to administer it, and has admitted that they frequently fed each other with *Alconut* — one would pop a piece into the other's mouth."

"As drinking wine with the arms intertwined." Felisa was in great fettle that night.

"Exactly!" Hardy had warmed to his part, as if each time he added to the list he felt more sure than ever that he had the right prisoner. "He was taken ill when he got home from the caravan — officially he was late home from the office and when he first complained to his wife he said that it must have been a sandwich he had bought at an all-night café at Charing Cross Station. She sent for a doctor soon after he reached home."

"Then surely she could not have poisoned him," I objected. "It would take some hours for the arsenic to take effect."

"He had a packet in his briefcase," Hardy replied. "He could have taken it from home. She — his wife — could have put the poison in there. But it looks more and more unlikely, Manny."

I was in Court when the judge sentenced Hilary Consett.

So was Benjamin Consett, her husband; he now had to return to his home and three children; make some plans to have them cared for. It could not have been a greater domestic tragedy; nor a more awful irony, for soon after she went to prison she inherited a substantial sum of money. Whichever way one looked at the affair, it was sad and distressing; and the possibility that she had been wrongly convicted always kept it fresh in the mind.

There was one thing I had not been asked either by Hardy or in Court. Was Hilary Consett a woman capable of committing such a murder, in my professional opinion? I was heartily glad that I was not called upon to say, because my answer could only have been: "Yes."

13

Meeting

OVER THE FOUR YEARS I HEARD A LITTLE ABOUT THE CASE.
Occasionally a journalist would make a feature article of
it in one of the more sensational Sunday newspapers;
occasionally Hardy would give me a snippet of information: that Hilary appeared to be settling down in the prison
where she had been sent — in the south of England. Every
newspaper carried the story, two years later, of Janetta
Grey's second marriage to an architect named Marcus
Hunter. Once, Hardy told me that Benjamin Consett had
let the top half of his Victorian house to a middle-aged
couple, the woman of whom looked after the children, who
were ten, seven and a few months at the time of the trial.
Later, they went to join Consett's parents who lived in
Australia. Occasionally I had letters from Hilary Consett's
brother, who lived in California; he was the only member
of her family who consistently fought against accepting
Hilary's guilt.

I was taken completely by surprise when one day in July,
early in the fifth year of the sentence, he telephoned for an
appointment: would I see him and discuss other aspects of
the case. He said that he was asking for professional
consultation and help — not what he called a free ride. So
I told him what I would have told anybody in those
circumstances.

"I will be happy to discuss the case with you, Mr. Jees, and should you convince me that there is an angle which should be looked into again, perhaps more closely, then there will be an appropriate fee. But I am not sanguine."

"Provided you'll keep an open mind," the caller said. "May I bring my wife?"

"Most certainly, if you wish. Perhaps you would care to come to tea . . ."

Felisa, I knew, would be more than agreeable to make one of her luscious Sacher cakes. England, moreover, is one of the few countries where one can still obtain cream of the right consistency to whip for this and other continental delicacies. And provided she sat still and did not interrupt, conquering all her impulses to, and provided she was not asked by the Jees to leave, she would be in high delight.

It is my custom when receiving strangers to ask Felisa to admit them and to lead them to the sitting-room, a museum-like room which can. overawe some people; in fact their reaction to the room is fascinating and often a guide to their attitudes and sense of values. It is not a dark room but the walls are papered in a dark pattern, and some bookcases as well as some display cabinets are against the walls; each can be lit by concealed fluorescent lighting, to show the figurines and the tiny *objets d'art* on the velvet-covered shelves.

In the middle of the room, which overlooks some heath-land, and trees and shrubs, like a miniature Hampstead Heath or Wimbledon Common of the kind which abound in my adopted city, is a cabinet containing three golden caskets, each handwrought by the great Cellini of the Italian Renaissance period; I have been assured but have no documentary proof that my family is in direct line from this artist of such consummate skill. It is a romantic conception and Felisa believes it absolutely.

These three caskets were rescued from a treasure which

my uncle once accumulated; most of the collection was taken by the Nazis but these were buried and, long after the war, sent to me as my uncle's sole legatee. Most of the other *objets* in the room had been given to me by patients whom I had helped and who wished to mark their feelings by more than my fee. Some, Felisa and I had collected as we had travelled about Europe.

To me, this was a room of yesterday and a promise for tomorrow.

I heard Felisa's silk dress rustling as she ushered the Jees in, assured them I would not be many minutes, and closed the door on them. The click of the door was the last sound for what seemed a long time. It was the man who broke the silence.

"Honey, it's like being at an altar."

"George," the woman said, "can those caskets be real gold?"

"If they're not real, he's a phoney," George said. "My! Did you ever see anything more beautiful? And honey — *look*!" I heard him move so he was heading for one of the cabinets. "They are original Dresden pieces — they — "

He broke off, and I left them for a few minutes, knowing that they so venerated what they saw that their concentration had been distracted from the reason for their coming. Before they began to talk, giving evidence that the mesmeric effect of the caskets and the *objets* was wearing off, I opened the door some way off and then approached this one so that they could not fail to hear me.

I liked them, immediately, and believe that the liking was mutual.

George told me that he simply did not believe his sister capable of the crime of murder ...

He repeated this in the living-room, sitting with Felisa's Sacher cake and wafer-thin bread-and-butter and tea in cups of the most fragile *Sèvres* china, which she took out only when most anxious to create a good impression. This could only mean that she had taken to the couple; and probably had been listening at the door to hear their comments about the room.

George said for what must have been the fourth time: "I simply don't believe Hilary capable of it, Dr. Cellini. That is what keeps me going."

"Mr. Jees," I said, "I don't agree with you."

"You mean you *do* think her capable?"

I could not tell him that yes, I meant specifically his cherished sister; but I could say with deep conviction and persuasiveness: "I think most human beings are capable of murder."

"But this slow, cold-blooded plot to kill — "

"We can all be cold-blooded in certain circumstances."

"I don't believe Hilary — "

"Mr. Jees," I interrupted, "I must make it very clear to you that if I carry out any form of investigation into the past of Mrs. Hunter — previously Mrs. Grey — I should have to press my inquiries to the full. I would ask permission to interview your sister, among others, and I have no doubt that it would be granted. If the results of my examination appeared to confirm her guilt, which would conversely help to establish the other woman's innocence, then I should have to say so in the clearest terms." I paused long enough to see the exchange of glances between him and his wife — who had said hardly a word — and went on: "Do you still wish me to ask Mrs. Hunter if I may examine her?"

Without hesitation, Jees said: "Yes. Just as soon as we can persuade her to see you."

It was a heaven-sent gift that Janetta Hunter did nothing desperate in the period which followed, although I did not know that until afterwards. They told me what they had seen of her; that they liked her; that she did not seem happy; that she was a very beautiful woman who looked younger even than her twenty-eight years; that she seldom seemed to laugh, that whenever they caught a glimpse of her she was staring into the distance, as if at visions which were hidden from others.

From time to time, either George or Esmé Jees telephoned me, about these and other things.

"We don't really like her husband." Whichever called, it was always a report from 'them'.

"She never has visitors."

"They never seem to go anywhere together."

"She can't be happy. *Could* it be because she has this awful thing on her conscience?"

"Or — is she unhappy for some different reason?"

"Marcus, we mean."

"We've tried to make him talk but he's a surly so-and-so."

"I think I've heard her crying," Esmé said, breaking from the 'we' at last. Then: "I'm sure I heard her crying."

"She seldom goes farther than the shops or the park by day, and even if she goes to Hendleton she's always back before he is."

"I don't — I really don't understand her. Dr. Cellini, can't we do something?"

"Wait," I urged. "Wait. But watch her closely."

I shall never cease being fervently relieved that I had advised that; or she might have killed herself, and the truth would never have been discovered; the burden laid upon me and others would have grown even heavier.

I was not wholly idle. What is the use of having friends in high places at Scotland Yard if one cannot sometimes call on them for help? I told John Hardy what I was doing, and he was intrigued; told me in the strictest confidence that the case still troubled him at times. But he had checked everyone involved, had cleared Benjamin Consett beyond all reasonable doubt; had made every effort to find out whether Anthony's death could possibly have been suicide.

"Have you checked Marcus Hunter?" I asked him.

"The new husband?" He was so startled that I knew his answer could only be 'no'. "It didn't even occur to me."

"Did he know Anthony Grey before he died?"

"There was no *affaire* between Marcus Hunter and Janetta," Hardy told me, so positively that I didn't ask him if he felt sure. "They didn't know each other." He had not 'checked' as such but had come upon certain information from certain zealous police officers. "I will check, but — " He shrugged his square shoulders, and looked into the distance. "It's a long time ago."

"Please try," I urged.

And I knew that he would; he was a thorough and astute man, although with his silver-coloured hair and fresh complexion he looked much more like a country solicitor than a senior officer at Scotland Yard. Within a week, he telephoned me to say with absolute conviction:

"Marcus Hunter and Janetta Grey did not meet until six months after her husband was buried. Hunter has always been a morose man, people who know him thought he was a misogynist and were astounded when he announced his impending marriage. On the strength of it he was given a ten per cent rise in salary, and was able to buy the house they live in at builder's price — he was one of the architects who worked on the Dingle Park Estate houses. What girl friends we've traced are well back in the past. He was an orphan, brought up by foster parents whom he hasn't seen for years. No one appears to like him," went on Hardy, "but everyone trusts and respects him."

"My, my, John!" I exclaimed. "You have been very thorough."

"Since you brought this up I haven't been able to get

Hilary Consett's face out of my mind," Hardy said, and then he added gruffly: "For that matter, I haven't been able to for a long time."

That was not at all surprising, for although Hardy and I had found her uninteresting compared to Janetta Hunter, she was a handsome woman, and statuesque, and with her olive skin and dark hair she looked as if she might have foreign blood. She had fine eyes, too, which could flash with scorn and light up — even in the dock; even, they say, in prison — with quick laughter. Everyone who knew her liked her, as far as the police were able to find out.

Had she murdered her lover, Anthony Grey I wondered, or had she been wrongly convicted?

It would not be at all true to say that I had a premonition about Janetta Hunter. I was uneasy about her because all that the Jees told me suggested that beneath her frigid calm was a volcano which could erupt with terrible violence; that what she looked into with her beautiful eyes was an inferno of self-torment and perhaps of torment inflicted from outside, conceivably by this Marcus. I was sure only of one thing: once she had reached the point of breaking, and only then, would she talk freely and truthfully. She had to be near breaking point before she would talk and I would explain this to the Jees so that they should understand that there was nothing dilatory in my attitude.

Then, one afternoon in July, my telephone bell rang, and by good chance I was home early, having appeared as a defence witness in a very sordid case, called on once again to express an opinion about a man's sanity: a murderer's.

"This is Dr. Cellini," I responded, hoping that I would not have to go out.

"Manny!" exclaimed George Jees. "She tried to kill herself. I stopped her. And she's talked like a fountain and I'm sure she'll talk when she sees you. And — " I waited, fully aware of the excitement in the caller's voice, sure that he had some news which he was certain would be devastating. "And she lied about not knowing of Hilary's *affaire* with her husband. She *knew* about that. Now you can't be so sure that she's innocent, can you?"

Excitement would obstruct objectiveness in George Jee's lively mind, but if this were true it did open up fresh possibilities. I had no doubt at all what I must do.

"If you will stay in, I will come and see you," I said. "And I would like all you can tell me in the minutest detail. The minutest, if you please."

14

One Hidden Fear

I COULD READ GEORGE JEES'S EXCITEMENT IN HIS EYES. In some ways very like his sister, I had always known that there was a streak of ruthlessness in him; that forced into a corner, he could be a dangerous man. Above all things he had always fought to clear his sister's name.

I thought about this as I drove first to Hendleton and then to Dingle Park. It was a warm evening, as warm as we had yet had. My car caught the attention it never failed to attract: from some, those who love old vehicles, and recognise them as works of art, a form of veneration; at least two caps were doffed. From some, ridicule; mostly these were young people to whom a 1930 model bull-nosed Morris-Cowley simply looked old-fashioned. I was appreciative of the first group and indifferent to the second. Whenever I had time I would polish the brass of the lamps and hand-bars myself, and I boast that there is not a better-kept car in London. Now and again I wondered whether I should indulge in a new car with automatic drive, but clutch and gear of this vehicle worked with smooth precision and the motor was surprisingly smooth.

There was another reason for keeping it on the roads: a great many people including policemen from senior officers to policemen on traffic duty recognised it, and in turn recognised me. There is pleasure in such recognition and occasionally privilege, too.

It was a little after eight o'clock when I reached Number 28 Henley Street, where the Jees lived; and almost as soon as the square-shaped car drew within sight of the window, George was striding towards me from the front door.

"Manny, you're a marvel!"

"If you will be good enough to tell me where to put the car," I said.

"Oh, you can leave it there."

I looked somewhat nervously at a group of early teen-agers at one end of the street and some younger children not far away; all seemed to be eyeing the ancient car. I did not hesitate, however, but left it at the kerb and followed George, saying:

"Has Janetta gone back yet?"

"Yes," George said. "She thought it would make her husband angry if she was out when he came from work."

"So." We were already at the door.

"She is terrified of him," George said.

"And I think she has cause to be," put in Esmé, who was just inside the passage, holding their large Dalmatian dog by the collar. I had never met but knew this dog by reputation. It was remarkably obedient, and sat in the window when all three of us were in the front room.

Esmé had made coffee, which was very good; and between them she and George told me the story of the day. Moreover, they told it well, drawing a picture of Janetta Hunter which made me sorry for the young woman before I had had a chance to talk to her.

There was something else: Esmé and George appeared deeply worried about her, and they were sure in their own minds that she was genuinely frightened of and in danger from her husband. Pressed to explain why they were so sure, they could not; an atmosphere rather than direct statement; expression rather than actual words. They were absolutely certain that she lived in fear, and the ostensible cause was her husband.

"And she *could* be goaded by conscience," George insisted.

"What will you do, Dr. Cellini?" asked Esmé very quietly.

"I do not yet know," I replied, "although I confess I would very much like an opportunity to talk to Janetta tonight without alarming or alerting her husband. But I understand he seldom goes out at night."

"Practically never," George said. "I suppose I might — " He broke off.

"You really are the most exasperating man!" rebuked Esmé. "Do you know a way to help, or don't you?"

"I thought I might visit them, and call the husband aside on some pretext," George told her. "But I can't think of a good pretext."

Now, both husband and wife eyed me. I was quite accustomed to the way they looked, as if expecting miracles. People often do expect miracles and never get them, certainly not from me. At the same time I was facing an inescapable fact: the frustration caused by ordinary, everyday things. It was quite apparent that Janetta was in the frame of mind to talk; possible that an hour with her, even less, would be invaluable. Yet her husband seldom if ever left her at the house alone in the evening, and George was quite right: a very good pretext indeed was needed if Marcus Hunter were to be distracted. The delay could be disastrous, or at least create an abortive situation; and it might well be a long time before another such opportunity presented itself.

"I have it!" Esmé cried. "George can go and say I need help, some female frailty, and get her to come here. And you can talk to her then!"

"Brilliant!" exclaimed George instantly.

"If she is really under this man's domination, then when she goes back it will be extremely difficult for her to maintain the deception." I looked about the room hopefully. "You do have a telephone here, I presume?"

"It's in the kitchen," Esmé replied.

"I would very much like to use it," I said, rising.

"While you're on the telephone I'll take Spots for his nightly walk," George declared, springing up.

"And I'll come with you," Esmé declared.

Neither of them asked me whom I was going to telephone, but each made sure I could talk in complete privacy, with no fear at all of being overheard. I was appreciative, particularly because I was so troubled. It was not, as I have I trust explained before, a matter of premonition: it was a matter of learning some of the facts and interpreting them out of a long and exhaustive experience. When they had gone, the dog leading the way breathlessly, I dialled the number of New Scotland Yard. John Hardy often worked late at the office and there was a reasonable chance of finding him there.

"I'll find out, Dr. Cellini," an assistant said, on hearing my voice. "Please hold on." I waited, looking about this small kitchen, brightly painted in many colours and with a diversity of what are sometimes called 'gadgets' seldom seen in an English home. I was particularly intrigued by a box-like article in pure white plastic, marked *Ice Crusher*, and by an electric can-opener screwed to the wood of the window itself.

Felisa afterwards told me she had spurned one for years, they were easily obtainable in England!

"Hallo, Manny!" John Hardy *was* in, and before I could speak he went on with hearty good humour: "Wherever it is I'm afraid I can't come tonight."

"John," I said, "can you make a telephone call for me?"

"It depends whom it's to and what it's about," he replied cautiously.

"Such a friend!" I decided to sound indignant. "Such faith you have in me!"

"I like this less and less," John said, at least half-seriously, then suddenly his tone changed. "Is it about the Hilary Consett affair?"

"Yes."

"I'll help if I can," John said quietly.

One has to know John Hardy to understand the significance of his change of attitude; he was only too well aware that I might ask him to bend certain provisions of the law in such a way that they would reach breaking point. In most cases he should, as a policeman, say no; yet he knew as well as I that unyielding adherence to the letter of the law could often do great harm. The humanitarian in him could influence the policeman.

It would where Janetta and Hilary were concerned.

"I need to talk to Janetta Hunter without the husband's presence," I told him. And before he could ask why I went on: "It is conceivable that she will retract one statement she made before, if she is alone."

"Can't her husband help her?" John asked gruffly.

"No."

"What do you want me to do?"

"Is there some way in which you can have him persuaded to leave the house for an hour or two?" I asked, and when he made no immediate answer I went on: "A case, perhaps, of mistaken identity. A man very like him is wanted for questioning. You could be very polite and apologetic, John, and of course you want only to talk to him."

I could hear John laughing, deep in his throat.

"Manny," he said, "you're an old scoundrel!"

"John," I said, "it is conceivable that a woman has been imprisoned for a murder she did not commit."

There was a pause which was prolonged for a considerable time; I wondered what particular difficulty or impediment he had seen and was examining. It would be unwise to push him, especially since I was as sure as I could be that he would say 'yes'. But I wished he would hurry. Then I heard his voice in the background and realised that he was talking to someone else; I heard him say quite clearly: "Will you arrange that at once?" A moment later his voice was strong in my ear. "How quickly do you want this, Manny?"

"I am within two minutes' walk of her."

"At once, then?"

"Please."

"Just a moment." His voice faded again but only for a few seconds; he came back almost before I was ready. "There was a nasty accident in Hendleton Broadway to-night — two people were killed, and several witnesses are needed. Our man at Hendleton will ask Hunter to go to the station about this; several others are already there, so he won't feel that he's being picked on."

"John," I said, "I know very little of this case, you understand, but I would not like the husband to take vengeance on the woman. And I am uneasy; there is some factor I do not understand. Could you please have men at hand when Hunter returns?"

"Are you sure you're just feeling uneasy? You haven't any cause to expect trouble?"

"I am troubled. And I assure you that directly I have

formed any conclusion or obtained evidence I will tell you."

"Thanks. Are you at a public call box?"

"No, I am at a house nearby. If this number could be called when Hunter is about to start on his way home it might be a great help."

"I'll arrange that," promised John; and I was as sure as I could be that he would do everything he had promised. I read him the number, which I could see with some difficulty, and then went back to the front room, with its gay colours and its bamboos, the cushions on a bamboo chaise-longue, the Japanese scrolls on the walls, and looked about me.

I was seeking something which did not fit into the circumstances, without yet knowing what it was. Teased, as by a word on the tip of my tongue, I stood in the window, looking into the street over which the dusk was falling, softening the stark outlines of the box-like houses, and quietening the tones of paint too harsh in the bright sunlight. The street was quiet, and no one was close to my car, where the brass glowed in the light from street lamps which had just been switched on.

What *was* wrong?

There was some factor in the situation as I so far knew it which did not fit; or at least had not yet been explained. Such a realisation as this comes all too often and is most disquieting. It is one thing to form an opinion based on all the facts, but with one missing or wrongly presented, no positive opinion is possible, or, worse, one can make a wrong one.

Esmé came hurrying from the direction of the park; she waved to me and her smile was warm and bright. A moment later, from the front door, she called:

"Am I back too soon?"

"No, my dear."

"Have you arranged it?" Now she was in the doorway,

bright-faced and eager; I had not before noticed how beautiful was the copper colour of her hair nor how lithe the movements of her body. The impression both she and her husband gave was of complete physical fitness and well-being.

"Yes."

"You are a worker of miracles!" She came across and kissed me on the cheek; and hugged me. "Manny," she said with a catch in her voice, "you will never know how much this means to George. He — he worships Hilary."

Gruffly, I said: "So I understand, my dear."

And I stood blinking at her, not unaware of the attractiveness of her heart-shaped face. She wasn't beautiful as was Janetta Hunter, but she was attractive with the kind of natural seductiveness given to some women and often a great burden to them, particularly after marriage. Now she drew away from me, and looked just a little abashed.

"You *are* a worker of miracles," she said.

"At best, this is only a little one," I replied.

"Do you know what will happen?"

"Someone will come for Janetta's husband and take him off, and you will be telephoned when he is on his way back, in time to warn me."

"And you'll go to see her?"

"Yes," I said.

"Manny — " She began, only to break off.

George Jees had called me by this diminutive from time to time, and I was accustomed to it from others, but until this, Esmé had always been formal; now for the second time she used 'Manny' and I wondered what mood it indicated, for she was a most volatile person.

"Yes, my dear," I prompted.

"I always have — have a feeling that you are looking through me."

"I do assure you I am not!"

9—TMDIK * *

"And — *right* through George."

"Not even through George," I assured her.

"Manny — I love him very much."

"It is very evident that you do," I assured her.

"But he has his faults."

"Yes," I agreed. I did not know what she was trying to say but I did know that it might be important, if only because of her difficulty in getting to the point, a difficulty rare in her. And I added sententiously: "We all have our faults."

"He — tries too hard to be fair." She gave a little laugh. "I suppose it is the English in him!"

"I do not think that quality is particularly English," I replied, "but I know what you mean." In fact it seemed to me that I was beginning to understand beyond George's love of fair play; the English, whom I love and respect and admire in so many ways, *do* sometimes give the impression of thinking they have a monopoly of this virtue; when I was younger this smugness irritated me. "What are you trying to tell me, Esmé?"

She said: "He is so anxious to be fair to Janetta."

"So?"

"Manny," Esmé said, "don't you think she's the most beautiful woman you have ever seen?"

"No, my dear," I answered gently. "Beautiful yes, but I have seen — " I broke off, my eyes narrowing, and waited, for she had not yet finished.

"He — he is so anxious to be fair to Janetta that he has to make himself remember that he's doing this for Hilary," Esmé said. "He — he was deeply impressed by Janetta on their first meeting."

"Ah," I breathed.

"Almost too — " she began, and then she backed further away, raising clenched fists to her bosom, and in a broken voice she went on: "Oh, I hate myself for saying this! Sometimes I think he is in love with Janetta, that at heart what he really wants is for you to prove she didn't kill Anthony Grey. Haven't *you* noticed how intense he is about it?"

"Yes," I said, "yes." And I saw what might be the missing fact: the piece I needed for the puzzle. "Too intense you think for his interest to be solely for his sister's sake?"

"Yes," she almost sobbed. "Yes, he — " She broke off, tears flooding her eyes. "He's been obsessed by the need for coming back. Until I came with him and saw Janetta and discovered how he behaves over her, this possibility did not occur to me, but now it haunts me. That he really came back because he couldn't keep away from Janetta."

I was quite sure of one thing: this fear, so cleverly hidden, was deep in her. I was as sure that I had to examine George's actions and all he had told me and would tell me in the light of this new understanding. There was nothing helpful I could say now, and words of empty comfort would not help.

I was relieved of the need of using any words at all, for a large car drew slowly past the window and almost at the same moment George turned into the gate, Spots for once hanging back. Esmé moved towards the open door as George's key sounded in the lock, and almost as soon as the door opened he called:

"There's a police car outside Janetta's place."

"Manny has worked a miracle," Esmé said, with a smile so natural one would not have dreamt she had any anxiety on her mind.

We were all together in the front room, sitting without lights, when the big car passed in the other direction. I did not know Marcus Hunter but had no doubt who the big man in the back of the car was.

"There he goes," George said, and then added in a voice of restrained eagerness: "Would you like me to go and prepare her for you, Manny?"

"Thank you," I said, "but I think I would do well to introduce myself."

15

Encounter

JANETTA HUNTER WHOM I HAD KNOWN AT THE TIME AS Janetta Grey, recognised me the moment she opened the front door. There was light behind her, street light and the last glow of dusk in front of her, combining in a trick of light which made her quite breathtakingly beautiful. She stood with a hand on the door, as if to bar my entry; and I had no doubt that the moment she saw me she knew why her husband had been sent for.

"Good evening, Mrs. Hunter," I said. "I am Dr. Cellini."

"I know," she said, "I know. I saw you at the trial." She did not move at first and I wondered if, after all, her mood had hardened so that she did not wish to talk. Then slowly she lowered her arm and stood aside. "Please come in."

"Thank you."

"The second door, please."

This second door led into a small dining-room, and the spare contemporary furniture, the design paintings on the walls and the lack of colour gave an impression of austerity particularly vivid after the colourful brightness of the house I had just come from. The furniture was so arranged that two angular-looking armchairs were in one corner turned towards a television set which appeared to have been built into the wall.

"Can I get you some coffee?" she asked mechanically.

"There is nothing stronger in the house. My husband is a teetotaller."

"If you want a drink — "

"No," she said, and unexpectedly gave a smile which lit up her whole face. "Unless you think it would help me to talk!"

I found myself chuckling.

"Would it help you?"

She hesitated for a few moments, looking at me searchingly. The smile faded, her expression grew sombre. I returned her gaze, not uneasily but acutely aware that I had seldom been scrutinised in such a way; it was as if she were seeking in me some quality she found elusive. We stood like that for a long time before suddenly she smiled again with that radiance I found so unexpected, and said:

"Come into the kitchen with me, and I will make some coffee. Or would you prefer tea?"

"Thank you, coffee will be excellent." I followed her into a kitchen so spick-and-span it might have been a model kitchen in an exhibition. All the pans were of steel; they shone. The hanging cooking instruments shone, too. There was no blemish that I could see on the colour washed walls and the pale woodwork. The stove and a refrigerator were built in close to the sink. She had obviously prepared a percolator for the morning and simply plugged it in. Then she opened a head-high cupboard and took out a canister marked 'Biscuits'. "Did you arrange for my husband to be taken away?"

"I arranged for him to go to help the police in their inquiries over a very distressing accident," I replied. "Not taken away. He will be back before long."

"So, we should hurry," she retorted drily.

"Not unduly," I assured her. "What we have to do should not be hurried, Mrs. Hunter. I was anxious to see you tonight because it seemed possible that you were frightened to stay here alone with your husband."

After a very long pause, she answered with quiet vehemence: "Sometimes I am."

"But not tonight?" Manny asked.

She hitched herself up on a kitchen stool, a graceful movement, consciously or unconsciously drawing attention to her figure and especially to her legs. She wore a sheathlike dress of a pale brown which did not now cover her knees. She smoothed the skirt down and then motioned to a folding chair close to me, and I sat down; it was very firm.

"I don't know what's got into me tonight," she said, and when I simply raised my eyebrows she went on: "I think it must be because I talked to the Jees."

"Ah," I said.

"Have they told you what I told them?"

"Yes."

"That I lied about not knowing about Anthony and Hilary?"

"Yes."

"Will you have to tell the police?" she asked, without a tremor in her voice.

"I may have to," I replied. "You may wish me to." When she made no comment I went on: "Do you feel less troubled?"

"In a way, yes," she said. "It may be because I told the truth about that. It may be because I talked to them and — and feel among friends." She paused but I did not comment, so she in turn went on: "Or it may be because I know that if it comes to the worst I am really capable of killing myself. Doesn't that sound awful?"

"It sounds true," I said.

"And you worship the truth, don't you?"

The coffee was beginning to make a little burping sound

but neither of us looked towards it; a clock was ticking but I could not see it.

"Do you know, I had never thought in terms of worshipping the truth," I replied, leaning back against the wall. "I really hadn't. I venerate any truth which will help a human being. I am in no way averse to white lies, such as your husband has been told tonight. I think if we could base a society on it we would be a much happier people — if we could be sure that no one lied to us about anything, that we could take everything we are told as the literal truth — "

She interrupted me with a laugh. She was behaving so differently from what I had expected that I wondered whether it were possible that she had taken drugs. Yet her eyes were clear and there was nothing in her manner even to hint at that.

"I'm sorry," she said. "Oh what a tangled web we weave when first we practise to deceive."

"I beg your pardon?"

"And I'm sorry I'm being obscure, too," she went on. "Scott's old adage *did* spring into my mind. It did into yours, didn't it?"

"Something very like it," I admitted.

"Adage, axiom, cliché! I am always shuddering at my husband for using them, and suddenly I've realised that nearly everybody does. And I'm sorry if I seem hysterical, too." She frowned suddenly and stared at me, obviously waiting for a response.

"Hysterical is too strong a word," I said. "Light-hearted, perhaps."

"For me to be light-hearted *is* hysterical," she retorted, putting her head on one side. "I was waiting for you to say that I am not in the least bit hysterical, in which case I would have proof that you tell white lies — if lies told to deceive *are* white."

I said, quite simply: "I shall not deceive you."

"No," she said slowly. "I don't believe you will. What do you want to know? In addition to the fact that I lied when I said that I didn't know that Anthony had a mistress, a Venus of a woman named Hilary."

"You knew who she was?"

"Only vaguely."

"Why did you lie about knowing he had a mistress?"

"To try to avoid being accused of murdering Anthony."

"*Did* you murder him?" I asked quite flatly.

In a few seconds the whole atmosphere had changed; from warm to cold; friendly to hostile; happy to distressed; from relaxation to tension. What lived in this woman now showed: fear. But it was controlled fear now; wariness, too. I did not really know what answer to expect. One can worship at the altar of truth and turn away and utter the blackest lie, especially if it is to save oneself, or to save someone beloved.

Her eyes, I then discovered, were violet; and they could look black. A spot of light near the centre was deep violet, now.

At last, she replied: "I don't know."

"Janetta," I said gently, "that is not very convincing."

"Nevertheless, it is the truth as far as I know it."

"You know how he died?"

"Yes."

"Do you really believe that you or anyone else could obtain arsenic, place it in some chocolate, a task needing a steady hand and a great deal of concentration, then put the chocolates in a desk or a pocket and — *forget*?"

Without a moment's hesitation she said: "Yes."

"Yes what?"

"I do believe I could do all that and forget."

"I have had much experience with sufferers from amnesia

and am more easily persuaded than most, but even I find this hard to believe."

"So would the police," she retorted. "That is why I did not tell them. But then — " She broke off.

"Please go on."

"It doesn't matter," she declared.

"Anything held back, hidden or concealed could matter," I insisted. "And could matter very much."

Her gaze challenged me.

She had shifted her position a little and so the violet in her eyes showed much more; a velvety colour reflecting the light. She sat very still. I had no idea what she had been going to say and indeed it might prove to be a trifle of no consequence: what was of great consequence now was that she should tell me what it had been; that she should hold no conscious secrets and, by the release of all she really knew, perhaps open the gates of what lay hidden in the inner mind.

At last, she said: "I was going to say that you ought to know better than the police."

"Know what better?"

"How easily one can forget certain things while remembering others vividly."

"Or do you mean how conveniently."

"Please," she said. "Don't play on words."

"Janetta," I said gently, "I am not playing on words but on nerves and emotions, past and present. You say you can forget some actions — or at least not remember whether you carried out certain actions — and most people, even I, find that difficult to believe."

"*You* should not," she said challengingly.

I had not come prepared for her keenness of mind; for her forthrightness; for her readiness to attack me in her self-defence. So, I was unprepared for this vein of discussion and needed time to consider. She was so sure that I should not find it difficult to believe that she must be right, and I had overlooked some obvious factor, a familiar one, or at least one which I should not find it difficult to accept. She watched me, obviously knowing that I was probing into my own mind. The percolator was bubbling with restrained fury now, and getting louder and louder.

Suddenly, it stopped: had switched itself off. As suddenly, I knew exactly what she meant.

"Ah," I said. "There is a short gap in your life which you don't remember at all, and other periods where your memory is patchy. I have encountered similar cases, and would be prepared to examine you professionally to find out whether I think this is true of you."

Why that assurance should have brought a flood of tears, I do not know. This woman was full of the unexpected. She sat, ankles crossed, hands folded in her lap, tears filling her eyes and beginning to fall down her cheeks. It was just conceivable that she could control her tear-ducts, as some people — mostly children — can, and so cry at will, and there was no way in which I could be sure whether or not she was doing this. I felt sympathy but I showed none; I simply waited, with increasing tension.

Then she said: "Thank you." She slid off the stool. "I'm sorry — I just thought everyone would be so sure I was lying that they would never admit the possibility of that." She sniffed. "Do you — " She tore a towel off a roller over the sink and dabbed at her eyes and cheeks. "Do you take milk in your coffee? I can easily heat some."

"No. Just a little black coffee, please."

She poured out, and stood with two tall cups in her hands, eyes still moist but tears gone. She looked younger. She tried to smile but could not, as she asked: "Shall we go into the other room? The chairs are more comfortable."

"As you wish," I said.

"There's so much I forget," she declared. "And — sometimes I think I remember some things that happened, at others I think a whole period of my life is blank."

"A long period?"

"I simply don't know."

"Has anyone ever tried to help you to remember?"

"Goodness, no," she answered, and then went on with sudden bitterness I hadn't heard from her before: "All *he* wanted to help me do was submit to him."

"He?"

"Marcus. My husband."

"Did you tell him about this?"

"Yes," she answered. "Soon after we were married. And he's told me that I talked in my sleep about killing Anthony."

"Yet he urged you to forget."

"Commanded," she corrected, the bitterness darting out like a serpent's fang.

"He commanded you to forget what, exactly?"

"Everything about my previous marriage," she said. "And so of my previous husband. He would remind me of what he called my confession only when I tried to defy him."

Gently, I said: "That is not very understanding of him."

As we sat in those unexpectedly comfortable chairs, she said: "He is not very understanding."

"Did you tell him that you could not remember whether you had poisoned Anthony or not?" I asked.

"No," she replied. "I had no chance to go into detail. I simply told him that I forgot a lot of things that had happened then — I mean, about that period — and he told me that was over and done with, I must try not to think about it, must forget as much as I could."

"I see," I said. "Janetta, if you forgot many things that happened, how did you know that they happened?"

"I heard other people say they did," she answered.

"Can you give me one or two examples?"

"Yes," she said without hesitation, "there are dozens of them. I went to the bus with Anthony on the morning that he was taken ill, apparently. At — at one time, when we were happy, I always walked with him to the bus, but I hadn't done that for a year at least. I don't remember going with him that morning, but I must have. Several neighbours saw me, apparently, passengers who always caught the same bus. I do know this now, Dr. Cellini; the police made sure I knew."

"That is easy to imagine," I said, drily. "And another example?"

"That I cooked a special meal on — on that night."

"The night before you went with him to the bus stop or the night he came home sick?"

"The night he came home sick," she murmured. "I hadn't cooked a roast for a long time, or anything which meant preparation beforehand. I could never be sure he would be home, I *do* remember that. I always cooked a steak, or bacon and eggs or an omelette, but a roast was in the oven that night; I had not turned it off, and the oven kept turning itself on and off, apparently."

"Did the police tell you this?"

"A neighbour told me — one who came in when I rushed for help with Anthony. I *do* remember some things. She — "

Janetta broke off. I could see the underlying tension; the release from the relentless pressure she had exerted not to think still less to talk about these things, so I did not prompt her. The tears misted her eyes again but this time they did not fall, and the expression was of great pleading when at last she went on:

"Anthony came in late, and not well. Soon he had violent stomach cramps and groaned a lot, and I rushed for help. He was taken off in an ambulance to hospital, and died soon after arriving. I know all these things happened, they must have happened, but I don't remember his face or expression: I simply don't remember!"

16

The Hot and the Cold

SHE COULD BE LYING, OF COURSE; COULD BE SO ADEPT THAT
she fooled me enough to make me impatient with myself
because I permitted the faintest possibility of doubt, but
all that she said now sounded true and convincing. If she
had indeed forgotten a period of days, or even longer, then
it was reasonable that she would have no recollection of
poisoning the chocolates. If her memory was patchy about
that period, it was not unique. What was needed now was
to find out what was the last thing before the amnesia
period which she did remember, and what was the first
thing that happened afterwards and was clear in her mind.
This was the prior concern and I had no time or energy
to waste with anger at the fact that no one had attempted
to find out what had happened: that she should have been
so lonely for so long, damned by her own fears.

She was saying over and over again: "I don't remember,
I simply don't remember," as if she still felt the need to
convince me; so I leaned forward, holding out my hands;
and she took them.

"Do you want to remember?" I asked.

"Oh, yes, yes, yes!"

"And you want me to help you?"

"Yes, please, please, *yes*!"

"Even though you might remember doing these things for which Hilary has been imprisoned, and — "

"Yes," she said, gasping. "But — it isn't only Hilary." When I made no comment but only looked surprised, she went on: "You said you wanted the truth, didn't you? The whole truth and nothing but the truth? Well, that's *true*. I'm not concerned with Hilary, she doesn't really mean anything to me she's — she's nothing now. She took Anthony away and I hated her for that but I hated myself more. That is what I can never tell anyone about. I hated myself because I must have failed him. *Do you understand?*" she cried. "Or am I talking like a crazy woman? Am I *insane*?"

The grip of her fingers grew tighter all the time. She was leaning forward in her chair, her face upturned, her body at great strain. Her eyes were so violet it was like looking into pools of some liquid distilled from the flowers themselves. And one of her deepest fears was on the surface now, she had voiced a dread which must have terrified her.

"You are not insane," I said. "You are lucid and emotionally normal and I do understand. I also understand and may well be able to establish that you suffered from a period of amnesia. You must have thought about this a thousand times."

"I never seem to stop," she said.

"What do you last remember clearly?"

She said without hesitation: "The day before that day."

"What do you remember?"

"Waiting."

"Just waiting."

"Waiting and feeling so empty and so lonely."

"Waiting, empty and lonely," I said after her. "Nothing else?"

She began to breathe very fast.

"Angry," she said.

"How angry?"

"Very angry."

"With Anthony and Hilary?"

"And me! I hated myself. Here was I, young and beautiful and married to him and — and I'd lost him. I'd thrown
him away, I was viciously angry with myself."

"But also with them."

"Yes."

"Do you remember your feelings clearly?"

"As if I were going through them now," she said in a
strangled voice. "As if they were part of me."

"Janetta," I said. "They are."

She did not respond, except to close her eyes for a
moment; and one tear squeezed through and became a jewel
on her dark lashes; but did not fall down her cheek which
bore faint traces of the earlier tears.

"How angry did you feel at them?" I asked.

Without opening her eyes, she answered: "Angry enough
to kill them."

"Them."

"Both of them. I remember — " Her eyes opened to a
star-shot brilliance, and she slid from the edge of the chair
on to her knees, her face upturned in anger. "I dreamed of
killing them and killing them both. I saw no point at all in
living, I was a woman and yet so little treated as a woman,
I could not hold him, and she — oh, dear God, dear God,
how can you make your creatures so different? How can
you make some suffer so."

She placed her forehead upon my knees and began to
weep as I had never heard a woman weep. Her hands were
still in mine, no longer clenching; her fingers and her body
were no longer tense but limp. To help support her I sat
upright, and after a while my back began to ache, but I was
reluctant to disturb her, for I knew that the repressions of
years were pouring out of her. Eventually I had to shift my

10—TMDIK * *

position but not until the violence of her paroxysm had eased; and soon she was still, and silent; as she had been earlier with Esmé and George.

At last, she drew away and turned her face towards me. The tears in her eyes weakened the violet; the red at their rims took away the stars. She did not seem self-conscious, even when I took out a handkerchief, folded and ironed by Felisa, shook it at the corner and handed it to her. She dabbed at her eyes and blew her nose and then said "thank you" in a hoarse voice.

She looked at the small, silver-coloured wristwatch on her wrist.

"I am sure he won't be free for at least another hour," I assured her. "And I shall get warning when he is on the way, remember."

She nodded, and dabbed her eyes again.

"So I *wanted* to kill him," she said.

"A million people have wished very much the same," I told her.

"How many have done it?"

"Have you remembered that you did?" I asked sharply.

"No!" She was very emphatic. "But — I did wish them dead."

"Why?"

"What a ridiculous question!" The spirit was coming back to her and was good to see; she rose from her knees and went to her chair so that I could settle back in mine.

"All the same I would like an answer," I insisted.

"You know why! He had left me for her, she had seduced him — "

"Janetta," I said, "don't be silly."

"*What?*"

"Don't be silly. A woman of your calibre would never have such a motivation. It is cheap and melodramatic and old-fashioned. Will you please answer my question?"

She was startled, but behind that was something else, lurking; reluctance to tell the truth. I knew what it was by now, of course, and could have spared her this, but what to some might appear to be a humiliation would not, to her, for long. Besides, her confidante was an old man, wise in the ways of man and woman and sex and its variations, its strange permutations. Despite my tone, I was — for the first time — beginning to be really sorry for her. To be given such beauty and such a body and to find the body such a mockery.

She said: "You know the answer."

"I am too often wrong to be sure."

"I *think* that was a lie," she said. "You *think* you know the answer."

"Yes."

"Tell me and I will tell you if you are right or wrong."

"I would rather you told me," I said.

"To cleanse the spirit and purify the soul?" she mocked.

"To exorcise the devil," I retorted.

"Oh." She actually smiled briefly, and relaxed even more. "Yes, the devil. Do you believe in him?"

"Anything which tortures the human spirit is to me a devil," I said.

"You know, Dr. Cellini, you are very clever and you can be very evasive. I think you sometimes stretch this truth you worship."

"Stretch perhaps, but never break."

"You do know," she said. "I am not as other women are."

"That is not true," I countered.

"I cannot satisfy a man's carnal appetite," she stated.

"Some men's," I said.

"I have tried with only two. Do you believe that?"

"Yes," I told her, unhesitatingly.

"Thank you."

"It may be the basic cause of all that has happened," I continued.

"My failure to — "

"Your inexperience."

"Oh," she said, and glanced away and then looked into my eyes again; in hers the violet was back, a deep pool in which a man's mind could swim. "I have never been able to discuss it." She hesitated, and when I gave no sign, she added: "Sex."

"The sexual act."

"Yes."

"There is no need to discuss it. There is need to accept it as a natural practice between a man and a woman and — whatever the world may say, sometimes between woman and woman and man and man. Are you a lesbian?"

"No!" she almost gasped.

"You are too easily shocked," I said. "You were going to tell me why you wanted to kill Anthony and Hilary and then yourself."

"God knows it's self-evident now!" she cried.

"Janetta," I said, "you are a beautiful woman and you are undergoing a period of great emotional strain, but you are far more self-controlled than to start invoking the deity to be your witness, and far too cognisant with what I am trying to do to want to be coy."

She swallowed painfully. "I hated Hilary because she was able to have children, and myself because I was so frigid. Oh, yes, my being unable to have Anthony's child, and his turning to another woman, had *made* me frigid, I remember it all now. From the moment I knew, I couldn't bear him — *anyone* — to touch me. I still can't."

"Yes," I said, gently. "I can understand that. Did he make you feel as if you were a freak, or some such thing?"

"Some such thing," Janetta admitted, and my heart ached at the hurt in her eyes. "Dr. Cellini," she said, "I think I could love you very much."

"I think that *you* need very much to be loved," I told her quietly, and hesitated. Sometimes a casual phrase, or one dropped into a dialogue with seeming casualness, can be more effective than a closely reasoned statement of a case, which so often sounds like hectoring. The phrase, perhaps hardly noticed at its utterance, will often lie dormant for a while, like a seed in fertile ground, until it is watered by the need of it; and once watered, cultivated by the new hope it can offer. Was this the moment for such a phrase? She was waiting for much more, and did not prompt me, so I said quietly and yet I hope with seeming casualness: "I have known many women who cannot have children. Often this inability is temporary. As often, their reaction to what they mistakenly feel is a fault in themselves is similar to yours. But this reaction will pass." As she understood what I was saying her expression changed to one which might have been incredulity; but before she could dwell on it I hurried on: "You are not a freak. In my experience as a doctor, I would say that at some stage in their lives two women out of three feel as you do. Now! We have established a motive for you to kill Anthony, have we not?"

She nodded. "Yes."

"Good! And opportunity."

"Yes."

"And the mood."

"Yes."

"Did you ever buy any arsenic?"

"No," she gasped.

"Not even in weed-killer?"

"We never used weed-killer, it was such a tiny garden."

"Very well," I said, and switched to my earlier line of questioning.

"And you have no recollection of putting poison in the chocolates?"

"No, no, no!"

"We know however what preceded the amnesia — the day before, at all events. Next morning you walked to the bus with him. Where did you live?"

"On the other side of Hendleton. But I don't remember going to the bus!"

"Do you remember waking up that morning?"

"Does one *ever* remember waking up on any particular morning?" she demanded, but she was beginning to frown.

"Yes," I answered, "if the reason to remember is strong enough. One may remember waking on the day of a disaster, for instance — "

"This day was a disaster!"

"This day could be salvation," I told her sternly.

The word 'salvation' startled her. She looked on me with that strange brooding expression and for a few moments was absolutely still. Too still. Yet there was movement in her eyes as if they showed the wild turmoil of her mind. I was sure that she had remembered something; not at all sure what it was, except that it raged in her. She looked away as if afraid that I could see through her eyes to that seething vortex in her mind. Then, without warning, she swivelled her gaze back towards me and said:

"I remember the night before."

When I was sure she needed urging I said: "What happened then?"

"We quarrelled," she said flatly.

"You and Anthony quarrelled," I said. "A husband and wife — "

"No!" she gasped. "No!"

She was not shouting at me but at the thing she now

remembered. The quarrel. How it must have raged. And how it tore her, so that her face was distorted in the pain that it created, and her body writhed and her arms and legs writhed and she began to strike out, not at me but at nothing, beating the air; and she cried in an anguished voice, time and time and time again:

"No! No! No! No!"

She leaped from her chair as if from some awful threat. She screamed: *"No!"* in a terrible voice.

Then she began to moan and shake her head, turning it from side to side and yet keeping her body still; a dead stillness. But her head went on turning from side to side and the moaning came from her parted lips, until it was not moaning but harsh breathing; each breath deep and laboured, hoarse and choking.

Slowly, the breathing stopped: stopped.

She stood rigid for a moment, nothing moving, not her eyes nor her head nor her arms or legs, nor her body. She began to sway; had I not sprung to my feet and supported her she would have fallen backwards. For a few moments I was desperately afraid that she had died in that furious spasm, but she was not dead; her heart was beating beneath my hand; and when I felt for her pulse I found it slow but steady.

I could not hope to carry her up to a bed, so I pulled the two armchairs together and rested her in one, placed a dining chair between them so that she could lie flat. I went into the kitchen where I had seen a cushion on the back of her stool, and brought it in to place beneath her neck. Next, I fetched a bowl of cold water and a towel from a rack, and bathed and dried and bathed and dried her forehead, her cheeks and her wrists.

All the time, her breathing improved until a moment came when there was a pause in it; and that was when I knew she had regained consciousness. She opened her eyes, narrowly, looking on the wrong side for me.

"I am here," I said. "And I am so sorry, Janetta."

She said in a ghost of a voice: "I remember what happened, now." Her gaze held mine, and did not waver. "He was home early that night and I played to him and he ignored me, and I asked him to give me more attention, the attention that a wife deserved. And he said nothing, just sat and read a newspaper and pretended not to hear me. Then," Janetta went on in a flat tone, "I began to shout at him and accuse him of sleeping with this other woman, of neglecting me for her, and — and he seemed to go mad. He seized me and he carried me upstairs and he — raped me. He raped me. And he shouted at me and screamed and asked me if this was what I wanted, or did I prefer to be neglected."

For a few moments, Janetta was silent but soon she went on in that flat, weary voice:

"Afterwards, we began to talk. We had never talked like it before. He promised he would come home early the next night; I promised that I would cook him the finest dinner he had ever come home to. Then we slept, I in his arms. I saw him to the bus next morning and then went to buy the meat and vegetables, everything needed for the celebration dinner. Celebration!" she exclaimed, and buried her face in her hands. "I had believed him when he said that he would never see her again, and that it was only me whom he loved.

"But — but he did not come home for dinner.

"He was as late as ever.

"And as I waited for him I came to hate him."

She stopped, opening her eyes fully to meet mine. She must have sensed the question that I wanted to ask but she did not answer it before it was uttered, simply waited for me to ask.

"Janetta, now that you remember so much more, tell me this. Have you now any recollection of poisoning the chocolates and giving them to him? Did your hate begin earlier than you have said?"

It seemed a long, long time before she answered; I began to fear, too long.

17

Can Memory Lie?

DESPITE ALL THE CRYING, ALL THE TORMENT, ALL THAT HAD happened to her that day; despite the tear stains on her cheeks and the smear of lipstick at her mouth, she looked so beautiful. And she no longer seemed remote, the brooding look had gone and yet I was sure that her mind was working.

I did not ask the question again. It was out, and only hers to answer.

At last she answered, very quietly: "No."

My old heart turned over, because I was so glad; I had been heavy with fear because she had delayed so long. My joy, indeed elation, must have shown in my expression, for she held out one hand and smiled up at me.

"No," she repeated. "I did not. But — "

But.

How could there be any qualifying of that answer? It had to be a straight yes or no, and now she was clouding the issue, and destroying or at least dimming my trust in her.

"But I learned about the Alconut chocolates that night," she said.

Here was a valid 'but', thanks be!

"Indeed?"

"He had an opened packet in his pocket," Janetta said

very positively. "In his right-hand pocket, it fell out when he was — when he was tearing off his clothes."

I could picture what had happened; yet I could not imagine her, emotional and overwrought, noticing that anything fell, never mind what pocket it fell from. But her expression was free from duplicity, there was something very childlike in her then.

"He told me — afterwards," she said. "When — when we were tidying up the room and getting ready for bed. I found them, he looked so guilty and ashamed — and then he told me that he and Hilary both loved these and shared them on their evenings together." Her eyes looked brighter now. "He asked me if I would like to try them and I laughed and said no thank you, and asked him where to put them. 'In the right-hand pocket of my jacket', he replied. 'A packet just fits in there but won't fit in the other side.' And I knew why," she went on, softly. "He had jagged the left-hand pocket on a nail, and I had to make the opening slightly smaller so as to hide the mending stitches. We laughed about that, too."

I, Manny Cellini, felt absolutely convinced that she was telling the truth, and it was a good thing to feel. I did not want to spoil her mood and yet I had to take the risk, and the longer it was delayed, I reasoned, the more harm it might do.

"You say you actually put the chocolates back?"

"Oh, yes," she said.

"You didn't eat one?"

"No," she answered. "That was the one thing I rebelled against: eating the kind of chocolates they shared. Isn't that silly?"

"No," I said. "Janetta — "

"It's true," she assured me, and as she sat up, easily, smoothly, she had never seemed more confident. "It's absolutely true, Dr. Cellini, I've remembered so much detail, if I had put poison in those chocolates I would remember. Listen!" she exhorted. "I kicked against them on the floor, with my bare foot, then picked them up. Anthony looked as if he could fall through the floor! Then he told me why and offered me one, and when I said 'no' he told me to put them in his pocket. That's the simple truth. Now that I do know it, you must believe me."

"Yes," I assured her. "I believe you."

"So I didn't kill him," she cried. "Thank God!"

"I am quite sure you didn't kill him," I assured her with deep conviction.

"So it must have been Hilary! And if it was Hilary then everything's all right — or as all right as it can be now that Anthony's dead. I needn't doubt myself any more, I needn't live under a cloud! It's something to rejoice about — truly to rejoice!" She was on her feet now, close beside me, and to my surprise she put her arms round me but instead of kissing, as had Esmé, she gazed appealingly, imploringly into my eyes. "Oh, please," she begged, "*please* be happy. *She* must have killed him, justice has been done!"

I knew exactly how she was feeling, was touched with her elation but also touched with a fear which, once she shared it, would cast her down. Should I tell her of those doubts now, I asked myself? Should I spoil her joy even though it could only be a short time before she might— she *would* have to know them and, later, they might do her more harm than now? It would take only a few days for the excitement to fade, and she would have to face new problems then. Should she be made to grapple with them today?

I do not know to this day what decision I would have made, had it been left to me, but it was instead torn out of my hands and the need for a decision of another kind was thrust upon me.

For there came a sharp rap at the front door.

This would be George with word of Marcus Hunter's return, much sooner than I had expected. There would be little time for further talk with Janetta, unless she were to leave with me, so that her husband returned to an empty house. With the knocking she turned her head towards the window and undoubtedly she felt a stab of fear.

"Come with me," I said, taking her hand, and she followed me to the front door. I opened it, on an anxious George, who spoke before he could see us both.

"He'll be here in fifteen minutes — he's just left Hendleton." He saw Janetta behind me, and went on as if from the heart: "Don't stay here, Jan, come with us. You can't take your life in your hands."

"I would like to spend a little more time with Dr. Cellini," Janetta replied.

"But if you're coming with us you'll have to pack! There isn't any time."

"There is enough," Janetta said, calmly. "Will you stay for a little longer, Dr. Cellini?"

"Most certainly," I said.

"I suppose you know what you're doing." George sounded almost sulky, and then suddenly his voice rose and he rounded on me. "Do you know what a savage brute her husband is? Do you realise he might injure her for life, might even kill her? You've got to let her come with us. *You* can talk with Marcus, he might listen to you."

"George, we're wasting time," Janetta said.

"Wasting — " began George, then he turned on me again and spoke in a low-pitched, angry voice: "Don't let her stay. Understand? If she comes to any harm it will be your fault, and I'll see the whole world learns about it!"

"If you raise your voice much more," I protested, "the world will know sooner than you intended."

George drew in a sharp breath. His fists were clenched, his good humour had gone completely and he was as belligerent as a man could be.

"Look after her or I'll make you pay for it, understand?" He glared at me for a few seconds, then turned on his heel and went out. Janetta, looking pensive, led the way back to the room we had come from, while I seemed to see and to hear Esmé, telling me what George felt about Janetta.

Inside the room, I asked: "*Are* you frightened of your husband?"

"Yes," she answered quietly.

"At the risk of losing precious time, what is the real reason?"

She said quietly: "Because he can be so brutal. Because he looks upon me as a possession. Because he — he has handled me as Anthony did not once but many times." She stood so small and fragile-looking in a corner opposite the door. "It didn't matter so much because I've never been in love with him and — and I *have* nearly driven him out of his mind."

"Because you have been as frigid with him?"

"Yes."

"Do you think you could change?"

"With Marcus?" She actually laughed. "No, it would be quite impossible. He really does believe women are chattels, little more than slaves, he would have been better in a land of concubines. Anthony was frustrated but — " She broke off, glancing at her watch; and once again she forced a smile. "You were going to say something when George came," she reminded me. "What was it, please?"

After a few moments in which I felt a strange tension, I asked:

"Did you love Anthony?"

"At one time, very, very much."

"*Do* you love Anthony?"

"His ghost?" she asked. "His memory? The what might have been?" She hesitated and the smile played softly about her lips. "No," she answered at last. "No. He is dead and even after what I remembered my feeling is dead. No, I don't love Anthony's memory or Anthony's ghost. Why?"

"Because he might have brought poisoned chocolates home to poison you," I said. "And after the reconciliation could not face Hilary and could not face you. So, he chose his way of throwing himself in front of a train."

She had that trick of stillness developed to a remarkable degree, and it had never been more effective or dramatic than it was in those few moments. She was so still that she seemed to stop everything: the ticking of the clock, the beating of my heart. We had so little time left, and yet the seconds flew and neither of us spoke or moved, until she said:

"Do you really think that?"

"It is a very real possibility," I told her.

"Yes. I — I suppose so." She moved at last. "Can we ever prove it?"

"I shall not know unless I try," I said. "If he did — "

"Hilary should not be in prison."

"No," I agreed.

"Any more than if I had killed him."

"You are quite right," I said.

"*Will* you try to prove it?"

"I think I must," I said, and have no doubt that I sounded weary at the prospect of such a task. "I am sure I must," I added, more briskly. "Quite sure."

"Dear Doctor Cellini," she said. "You really are a darling but I'm not at all sure that Esmé was right." Before I could ask 'in what way?' she gave one of her unexpected smiles, and touched my lips with her fore-finger. "She thinks you are the wisest man she's ever known."

"Whereas you, much nearer the mark, think I am the most foolish," I rejoined. "Janetta — we have no more than five minutes, my dear."

"I know," she said.

"What are you going to do?" I asked. "Come with me? You do not have to stay with the Jees, you will be very welcome at my home and my wife already has a healthy curiosity about you. Or will you stay and see Marcus?"

"What do you advise?" she asked.

"That you should do what you feel that you must do, of course."

"The master of evasion," Janetta said, over a laugh that sounded almost carefree. "Shall I run away again?"

"I have known people who have run away all their lives."

"Happy people?"

"People," I replied.

She stood still again but now it was a different stillness, not fed by tension. She looked tired, I remember, and young and beautiful and vulnerable. The seconds were ticking by and I did not want Marcus to find me here, but we were not done yet: I had to see even more clearly into this woman's mind. She made a picture which is always vivid and always real to me. It was not for a long time afterwards that I really understood how I felt and why I felt so keenly about Janetta.

She was so very like Felisa had been in the days of her young womanhood.

"I think," she began, only to stop until she went on more firmly: "I shall stay."

"I can make sure he does not harm you."

"You mean — let him know you have been here?"

"Let him know you are no longer alone," I corrected.

"Yes," she said, smiling slowly. "I am not alone any longer, am I?" She put a hand up to my cheek and stroked just twice. "Thank you. Can you be near, in case I need you?"

"Yes," I promised. "With the Jees. But Janetta — "

"You might be in the next room and yet too far away," she said to me. "I do know, truly. Can you really be so near?"

"Yes. Will you really come for help?"

"Yes," she said. "If I cannot cope, I will come to you."

I believed her; yet I was afraid for her.

I believed also that some precious quality, faith, trust in herself, had been reborn that night, and might die in its infancy if she would not cope alone. I did not know what psychological weapon she had at her disposal but believed she had one.

"Please go now," she said. "And — thank you very much."

I saw the light in the front window of the Jees' house and could picture them just inside, watching for me, watching for Marcus. I did not go in at once. The narrow service alleys between the tiny houses were most convenient for what I wanted to do, so I slipped into the first one. I could, perhaps, have stayed four minutes, even longer with Janetta, but certainly not a moment more for a car turned smoothly into the street, its headlights dimmed, and I crouched back to make sure that I was not seen.

The car pulled up outside Janetta's house. Two doors opened, front and rear; the man at the front had a peaked cap, and was already by a split second in time to open the rear door wider and to say:

"Good night, sir."

Marcus Hunter did not respond, but strode towards the

front door of his house. He was a much taller and bigger man than I had expected and moved as if he were driven by a high wind. There was enough light to show his exceptional handsomeness, and I saw that he was dark and that his eyes had a baleful look.

He disappeared as the front door of the house opened and Janetta said in a clear, calm voice:

"Hallo, Marcus. I'm glad you're back."

I remembered how positive she had been when she had said that last night she could have killed him.

And I remembered how he had treated her; and his strength; and her new self-confidence.

It has always been my belief that man must, in the last account, best work out his own salvation . . .

BOOK III

Through the eyes of
JANETTA

18

The Beauty and the Beast

THE DOOR CLOSED ON DR. CELLINI, AND SEEMED TO SHUT
out a period of my life; a dark and menacing period. I
heard his footsteps, light and quick, until they faded and
I was alone in my own house; and yet I had never felt less
alone.

I had not killed Anthony. I could have shouted that
aloud; I had not killed Anthony!

I *did* shout it aloud as I went back into the dining-room,
and my voice echoed and re-echoed: *"I did not kill
Anthony!"*

I felt no crushing sense of burden any longer. I had
hardly any sense of fear: enough to marvel that I had so
little. I moved the two chairs apart and placed them in
their accustomed position and carried the coffee cups into
the kitchen. I was about to wash them up under the hot
water tap when something within me seemed to ask: "Why
do that? Are you still so frightened of him?"

I left them in the sink and hoisted myself up on the
stool; at eye level was a small mirror and I peered at my
reflection. No one could doubt that I had been crying. I
must dab on a little powder, put on lipstick —

Why? Are you still so frightened of him?

Aloud but in a subdued voice I answered: "No." And
added: "Not so afraid." On one side of the wooden top

section of the stove was a row of cooking utensils, among them a carving knife which I seldom handled; on the few occasions when I cooked a joint for the two of us, Marcus carved.

I took the knife off its hook, and smiled wryly: not *so* afraid was right.

I put the knife on the draining-board, not back on its hook, and sat with my ankles crossed and the heels of my shoes resting on the ledge of the stool, my hands in my lap, and reminded myself of the last things Dr. Cellini had said. Wise? Oh, he had both intelligence and cunning, and also a deep experience and a great love of people but above all he was wise.

And he worked miracles; he had brought back my memory; compelled me to face things which I had wanted above all to hide. I wondered why he had left me, and yet I knew the answer. I could make my life or break it; no one could make it for me. I had been lonely but now I was not simply, awfully lonely, I was on my own; my own executioner or my own —

Salvation.

I heard the car pull up outside; and had no doubt that it was Marcus. A door slammed and there were pounding footsteps, elephantine compared with Dr. Cellini's. I moved very quickly, and before he was at the front door, opened it and faced him.

"Hallo, Marcus," I said. "I'm glad you're back."

He did not speak, but paused, almost missing a step. I wondered whether he had expected to find the house empty and me gone. I moved against the wall and he pushed past; there was hardly room for the two of us. He went as far as the kitchen while I began to bolt and chain the door. Almost in the same movement he returned.

"I'll do that."

I stood aside, and let him. He rammed the bolt home

but the small chain was not so easy to handle, and he had to fiddle before he could get the knob into the channel. By then I was in the kitchen.

"Would you like some tea?" I asked. "Or — "

He strode towards me. "I would like to know what the hell you've been up to." He moved his hands, as if to drop them on my shoulders and in anticipation I could feel the weight; and the blows as they descended. But I backed away, much more nimbly than he expected and, red-faced with anger, he began again:

"I want to know what you've been — " and again he moved his hands.

"Marcus," I said, "if you so much as touch me I shall walk out of this house and never come back."

"You won't!" he rasped. "You wouldn't dare!"

I did not flinch away for this time he did not move to grasp me; his breath became shallow but he did not quite know what to do.

I said: "Oh, yes. I would dare."

He was baffled, and I well knew why. He had come storming, half-fearful of finding me gone but full of anger and knowing exactly what he would do if I were in: terrify me first into admission, then into submission. Oh, I had faced and defied him before but then I had been so afraid, and now I was no longer afraid, but full of confidence; and he knew, or sensed it; it was that which baffled him. He pushed his hand through his hair and for a moment looked as if he had been drinking.

"I'll break your neck before I'll let you go."

"You might have done, once," I said. "But not now."

"What the devil has got into you?" At least he stayed where he was, aggressive in voice but not in manner. "If you don't do what I tell you — "

"Not any more," I interrupted. "From now on I am myself again."

"What — " he began, only to break off as if the word choked him.

"I will tell you what has got into me," I said, very quietly. "Memory, Marcus. I have remembered what happened on the day when Anthony died. Everything. I did not kill him."

Marcus caught his breath.

"That makes a big difference, doesn't it," I said, with quiet confidence.

"You — you can't be sure!"

"Oh, yes. I'm sure."

"You can't be!"

"Marcus," I said, "I had a caller tonight, a man who — "

On the words, he lunged forward. I had known for a long, long time how ludicrously and yet dangerously jealous he was but I had not realised that the emotion was so strong that it could blind him, temporarily at least, to all reason. He used one hand to try to sweep the stool away and the other to snatch at me; but I was fully prepared and did not even hurry as I picked up the knife from the draining board.

"Don't," I said; and the blade caught the light.

He stopped, a hand on the back of the chair, the other in the air, the fist half-clenched; he would have buried his fingers in my hair had he reached me. The muscles in his neck and at his mouth worked; veins stood out on his forehead.

"Put that knife down!"

"I shall never be in doubt if I have to kill you," I said. "I should go straight to the police and tell them what I'd done."

"You've been to the police!"

"No I haven't."

"What did you tell them?"

"I haven't been to the police."

"You liar, you have! You pitched some story to make them take me into Hendleton, and you've talked to a detective here. What did you tell him?"

So it was fear, not jealousy, which had torn at his reason this time.

I held the knife by the wooden handle, lightly, in front of me. He glanced down at it, then back at me. His face was still working, he was at the threshold of one of the paroxysms of rage I knew so well.

"Do you really want to know what has happened?" I asked.

"If you don't tell me, I'll — "

"If you keep interrupting I won't tell you a thing."

His nostrils were distended; his teeth parted just enough for me to see the tip of his tongue. But he did not move except to lower his hands, and he was trembling from head to foot, as I had so often trembled.

"Tell me," he muttered.

"I saw a psychiatrist, who — "

"A psych — a bloody quack! Why, you little fool, if you believe — "

"I told him everything there is to tell about you and me," I said. "Everything."

"You darned little idiot."

"Marcus," I said, my patience strained as fear of him grew less, "abuse won't get you anywhere, it will only make you feel foolish. I told him everything, and he helped me to remember that I did not kill Anthony."

"But I heard you say you had! In your sleep, not once but three times!"

"Did you?" I asked coldly.

"You know I did!"

"I only know you say I said so, and have held that over

me for a year," I said bitterly. "If you hadn't, I would have left you a year ago."

"You'll never leave me!"

"Marcus," I said, "can't you get it into your head that I am not afraid of you?" As I finished he took a half-pace forward and my voice sharpened. "Stay there!" I raised the knife.

"My God!" he breathed. "You're insane!"

"Not any longer," I replied. "I have my sanity back."

"If I tell the police what you've said in your sleep — "

"I shall tell them what happened in such detail that they'll believe me," I answered with complete confidence. "There isn't any doubt, Marcus, so don't try to pretend that there is."

He stood back a pace — actually stood *back*. I could not believe that I had won so easily but for the moment there was no way of being sure and I kept my grip on the knife and watched him warily. His breathing was very shallow, and through his mouth, and when he spoke the words came with a rush, as if he had not the breath to say much.

"What do you want?"

"I want enough money to go away and live in comfort for three months," I said quietly. "That will give us both time to think over what has happened and make up our minds whether it is possible to start again." It was utterly impossible of course but I thought that this might be a sufficient balm to his wounded vanity to make him behave calmly, to remove all threat of violence. I could not be sure, could only try.

He echoed in a hoarse voice: "Three *months*."

"Yes."

"I can't afford it."

"Yes you can."

"Three *months* — it will seem a lifetime."

"It is the very least," I said.

He stood with his hands by his sides, scowling, still breathing through his mouth in that shallow, noisy way. He looked over my head once or twice and then to one side as if he were afraid of meeting my eye. Certainly the knife frightened him; so did my new confidence, to him utterly confounding.

"Janetta," he began, "can't we talk — "

"Marcus," I said, "we had the last talk we're going to have last night."

"I — I'm sorry about last night. I love you so much — "

"Marcus, don't come any nearer," I said, dropping my voice so that he must have known that I was deadly serious. "If you touch me I shall kill you. And no one who knows what life has been like with you could possibly blame me."

"You *never* said a truer word," said George Jees, from the dark shadows of the passage leading to the kitchen.

I was astounded.

Marcus swung round.

George came to the threshold of the room, smiling, almost gay but with a bleak look behind the gaiety and a hard note in the outward levity of his voice. Marcus was so astounded that after the one violent movement he neither moved nor spoke; but his breathing grew louder and louder, and seemed to come from all corners of the room.

"No one in the wide wide world could blame you, honey," George went on, "and the same world would be rid of one of its nastier specimens. You will be free at last, and I — "

Marcus leapt at him; and as he leapt I saw the knife flash into George's hand.

19

Killer—Lover?

EVERYTHING HAPPENED WITH BEWILDERING SPEED; ALMOST in the time it takes to draw breath. One moment George had appeared as if from nowhere, yet proving by his words that he had been listening. The next, Marcus leapt and the knife flashed, only to disappear.

There was something awe-inspiring in what followed. Marcus moved like dark light towards one side and the knife blade, aimed at his stomach or his breast, cut through his jacket, and for a moment stayed there like a spike. Next, Marcus thrust out his hands and twisted his body and picked George up; as if he were plucking fruit from a tree.

I saw it; I did not and shall never understand how Marcus did it — but one instant their bodies were hurtling towards each other and the knife thrust was made, the next Marcus held George above his head, arms bent not because of the weight but because the ceiling was too low for him to be held at arm's length. George was actually pressed against the ceiling, Marcus pressing one hand high on his chest, the other low against his stomach. Facing downwards, facing me, there was the expression of a gargoyle on his face; and terror.

Marcus spun round.

I had known him move bewilderingly fast but never

with such speed; I had known and felt his strength but never known he had such strength as this. One moment his back was towards me, the next he faced me with George helpless above his head.

"Now look at him," he roared. "Now look at your precious lover before I break his body into little pieces. *Look at him, not at me.*"

I looked steadily at Marcus, and said more calmly than I felt: "He is not my lover."

"Don't lie to me, he's been here behind my back whenever — "

"He is not my lover," I said. "Put him down."

"I am going to throw him through the window!"

George gasped in a reedy voice: "Make him put me down, make — "

Marcus thrust him higher against the ceiling, making him bang his head; the crack was loud, and George drew in a shivering breath but did not speak again.

"Marcus," I said, "I didn't know he was there and he is not my lover. He is Hilary's brother."

"I tell you he — " Marcus began, and then he stopped, and the scowl vanished and his expression changed from fury to surprise and disbelief. "I don't believe it."

"I don't care what you believe — he's Hilary's brother."

"I am," gasped George. "I am, I — "

Marcus banged his head again, but this time more gently; and he continued to stare at me.

"Hilary's brother."

"Yes, put him down."

"What's he doing here?"

"He came to try to prove I killed Anthony."

"Why the hell should he do that?"

"To free his sister," I said, easily now. "Marcus, put him down, please. *I* want to know how he got in, just as much as you do."

"He's been skulking here — "

That was the moment when another voice sounded from the passage, a quiet and friendly and yet firm voice: Dr. Cellini's. I don't know why that affected me as much as it did; why suddenly my knees went weak and I began to tremble, all the strength and resolve drawn out of me. I stared past Marcus and his victim as Dr. Cellini said:

"He has not, Mr. Hunter. He came in here only a few minutes after you. I was outside and saw him. I was in this house for over an hour this evening and it is my fault that you were taken to Hendleton for questioning: I misled the police into believing you had seen the accident."

Dr. Cellini came into the room.

A larger man could not have squeezed by, but he did so with ease, actually bowed to me, and then, moving farther from Marcus, looked first at him and then up at George. I was almost sure that his white moustache twitched in a smile.

"Please put Mr. Jees down," he said.

"I'll break his neck — "

"That would be very foolish of you. There are police at the back and at the front and they would strongly disapprove."

"Police!" gasped Marcus.

"*Police?*" I breathed.

"Yes, my dear," Dr. Cellini said. "I had the strongest feeling that the situation would reach its climax tonight and I did not feel it wise to trust myself, or even you, to cope. As it is — "

"This swine tried to knife me," growled Marcus, still holding George up high.

"I have no doubt that others might feel the same about you," Dr. Cellini replied calmly. "However, he did not knife you." The handle of the knife was actually dangling from Marcus's jacket, buried up to the hilt. "And you are in no further physical danger from him or anybody else. Please put him down."

Marcus actually pushed George tighter against the ceiling in a kind of grinding motion, and said in a grating voice: "I'd like to pulverise him." Then he withdrew his hands and George simply fell; and falling, screamed; and my heart turned over for fear he would break his bones as he dropped.

Marcus steadied him, with a hand at his back, so that his feet flopped to the floor, and his knees sagged; Marcus withdrew his hand and it looked for all the world as if George were grovelling on his knees. In fact he crawled away until he reached the sink; and then he sat against it, looking like a bleached golliwog, hands flopped against the floor.

"Thank you," Dr. Cellini said. "I am Dr. Cellini."

"Are you this qua- this psychiatrist?" Marcus growled.

"I really don't mind if you call me a quack," Dr. Cellini said, and this time I was quite sure he smiled; I saw how pink were his lips behind the bushy white of the moustache. "Mr. Hunter, it was Mr. Jees here who persuaded me to see your wife. He persuaded me that this was necessary partly because she was in great distress and partly because he wanted to try to prove that she had murdered her first husband; there was, I am now convinced, a third and perhaps the only true reason." He glanced at George but George was hanging his head as if it hurt too much to lift it. "And your wife *was* in very great distress, largely because of you."

After a short pause, Marcus thrust his head forward.

"A man's wife is a man's wife."

"But not his slave nor any kind of possession."

"When I want telling of my rights — "

"Mr. Hunter, you most certainly need telling how to treat a wife," Dr. Cellini said in a tone of cold reproof.

"My strong recommendation to you is that you consult a psychiatrist and tell him exactly how you have been behaving. I imagine that you will benefit greatly from his advice."

"Who the devil do you think you are?" roared Marcus.

Dr. Cellini simply looked at him. Whether that look would have been enough to quell Marcus, or whether they would have found themselves in sharp conflict I shall never know; because there was another interruption, but this time not so startling although it was just as sudden: the front door bell rang sharply. Marcus turned his head as if glad of an excuse to look away from Cellini.

"Who the hell's that?"

"You could find out," Dr. Cellini remarked.

Before Marcus moved, however, I slipped past him into the passage. I was in a strange state of suspension and near-euphoria, a mood in which I had never known myself before. I needed to be away from the others, if only for a moment; there was something unreal about what had been going on, just as there was something unreal, or at least unfamiliar, going on in me.

The front door was open, and before I could see who had rung the bell, I heard Spots, panting; so this would be Esmé; holding the dog back. I pulled the door wider open and there she was, holding Spots on a short leash, and so half-crouching and looking up at me. At the kerb I saw a dark car with its lights on, and by the car, a man. So the police *were* out there.

"Esmé!" I exclaimed.

"Is George here?" she asked, anxiously.

"Yes, but — "

"I must see him."

"Esmé, he — he's upset, I don't think you should come in now."

"But I must see him!" she insisted, and there was a

different tone in her voice. The dog growled; it was almost as if she had given him an order. "Let me pass, please."

I might — I am not sure but I might — have let her go without any further effort; but I was certainly not trying any conclusions with Spots, and so I stood aside. I wished I could warn Dr. Cellini about the dog, and even Marcus: Spots would introduce a new element. Still holding the dog on a short leash, Esmé went into the kitchen.

I heard her gasp; heard her say: "George!"

The dog must have pulled himself free and rushed to his master, for when I reached the door Spots was over by the sink licking George's face, eyes, nose, mouth, in an orgy of affection. Esmé stood on the threshold of the little kitchen which with Marcus and Dr. Cellini as well as George and the dog, was already overcrowded.

"What — what's happened? What have they done to you?" Esmé went slowly, hesitantly towards George, who was trying to fend Spots off. "What on earth is going on?" she cried.

To my surprise Dr. Cellini said drily: "The last act, Mrs. Jees."

"Last act? In what? George — George, are you all right?"

He did not answer, but Cellini did, quite briskly:

"In a long-drawn-out drama, Mrs. Jees. Will you be good enough to tell me why you and your husband have lied so much about the reason for your being in England and the frequency of your visits?"

"Lied?" Esmé straightened up. "We haven't lied to you or anybody."

"Mrs. Jees," Dr. Cellini said, "you said that your husband came to England briefly during the trial of his sister, you said — or he said and you did not deny — that you yourself could not come to England until recently, because of illness; but that at last you were both able to come together to seek out the truth."

"And that *is* true! It's why we're here."

"It can't be true," denied Dr. Cellini with absolute certainty.

"But it is!"

"Mrs. Jees," said Cellini, looking now at George, whose head was raised at last and who was watching with rounded eyes and open mouth, "you have a very affectionate dog. It obeys you instantly, as it would only obey constant companions. You could not have had this dog in the United States; quarantine restrictions in England would mean that you could not have brought it into this country. You may go to and fro across the Atlantic frequently, leaving the dog here, but you most certainly spend a great deal of time in this country or you would not have the abounding affection and the unquestioned obedience of a very fine animal."

Throughout all this, George and Esmé were either looking at each other, as if in consternation, or else at Cellini with increasing dismay. If for no other reason all he said would have been convincing, but directly he explained his reasoning the facts stood for themselves. Marcus, outside all this, stared uncomprehendingly about him; he did have the good sense not to intervene.

"So we must return to the question: why *are* you here?" He paused. "What have you been doing in England? Why did you tell Janetta a tissue of lies? Why, indeed, have you been attempting to confuse the issue, Mr. Jees? You allowed the police and me to think you had only just come back. What have you been doing in England and why did you suddenly reappear in the life of Janetta Hunter and her husband?"

George began to stand up.

Esmé had not moved towards him.

The Dalmatian, clearly bewildered, first looked and then began to trot from one to the other, but they were so intent upon Dr. Cellini and the situation that they ignored him.

"I must of course make it clear that you are under no obligation to tell me but I am persuaded that the police will want to know when they know what I have come to believe. If the reason is a harmless, or even a lawful one, then there is no need for alarm, and I will gladly act as a liaison between you and the police. However — "

"George," Esmé said in a hoarse voice, "we've got to get away."

"You cannot get away," Dr. Cellini said. "And even if you command the dog to hold us at bay and escape the police outside you will not get far before the police catch up with you. Running away from the officers outside would be quite sufficient justification for them to search for you."

"George — " Esmé repeated, and the name was uttered like a sigh.

I had a strong feeling that Dr. Cellini was doing to them what he had done to me; trying to make them break down. But there was a conscious resistance to telling the truth, not a subconscious oblivion. As I stood there I felt rather than heard a movement behind me, and a moment later Marcus rested his hands on my shoulders. It was a long, long time since I had known such gentleness from him: in the days when he had wooed me . . . and when I had married him because he was strong and sure of himself, and I was so lonely, weak and afraid.

So we stood there.

"George — "

"Don't say another word," George Jees ordered her, sharply. "Don't say a word, don't do a thing. I came in here tonight because I believed Janetta's life was at risk — I came to save her. That's all — the beginning and the end. And I came here to Dingle Park to work on Janetta and make her admit that she had killed her husband. I couldn't think of any other way of freeing my sister and clearing her name. That's all there is to say — every word. Not all the Dr. Cellinis in the world can prove anything different."

He stopped; and no one spoke. He moved a hand towards the dog who sprang to him, caught its collar, and began to move towards Esmé and the passage. Marcus's hands pressed more firmly but not painfully on my shoulders. We were nearer them than Dr. Cellini was; if they were to be stopped then we would have to stop them.

George took Esmé's hand with his free one; had the dog on one side and Esmé on the other, backing into the passage. The silence had a strange quality; it seemed to scream. Dr. Cellini, so small and yet distinguished, stood very still, and I wanted to shout at him, to tell him not to let the others go until I fully understood all that had happened and was happening now.

Suddenly, he spoke in his gentlest voice:

"Mr. Jees, tell me one thing."

"Not a word, to you or from you. Esmé, you go first."

"Just one thing," insisted Dr. Cellini. *"Why did you kill your sister's lover? Why have you allowed her to languish in jail for so long?"*

The only sound which stirred the silence came from Esmé. It was only a whisper, and just two words.

"Oh, God."

20

Motive

"Oh, God."

The whisper seemed to hover about the room and never wholly to fade. The woman was behind George, who still held the dog on that tight leash, half-crouching. I could not doubt the significance of the whisper: it was like a confession, or an admission: that Dr. Cellini had asked the question which mattered most; could do these two much harm.

Marcus, apparently affected, removed his hands from my shoulders; and I missed the warmth.

"Don't push me," George said in a strangled voice.

"Could it have been an attempt to murder Hilary?" Dr. Cellini asked in a dispassionate voice. "How much will you inherit from her when she dies?"

"No," Esmé gasped. "No!"

"Get him!" George Jees cried, close to the dog's pointing ears: and quick as light the Dalmatian first bounded and then leapt towards Dr. Cellini, who stood like an accusing angel, yet who flinched and thrust his hand outwards as the dog leapt.

Alone he would have been helpless, lacking the strength to fend the creature off; would have been seized and mauled, perhaps to death, had Marcus not gone forward. For the second time that night he moved as fast as I could imagine, reached the dog actually in the middle of its leap, holding it with both hainds round the belly as he had held its master; but this time his grip was gentle. Careful not to hurt the animal, he hugged its back against him as it turned its head to bite, snarling in frustration; but the holding hands were out of reach of the white teeth, the thrashing legs and the heaving body were unable to get free.

George spun round and rushed out, calling: "*Esmé, Esmé!*" but she didn't go with him. She leaned against the wall, as if helpless, face buried in her hands, hands hidden by the cascade of burnished hair. Men shouted, outside; footsteps thudded, a car door slammed, a police whistle shrilled. And while these things were happening Marcus looked round at me and said:

"Open the cloakroom door."

I hesitated, not understanding; then moved as what he intended to do dawned on me. I flew past Esmé, towards the door between the dining-room and the kitchen and opened it wide; there was barely room to turn round inside, but it was large enough for what he wanted. I saw him dump the dog, hind legs and tail, alongside the W.C. pan, so that it had nothing on which to grip and spring right back, and I backed quickly away as he took out the key, slammed the door, then for safety's sake locked it. The frenzy of barking drowned all other sound, and no one but its master or its mistress would be able to quieten the fury.

Esmé was still in the same position.

I wanted to ask her: "Did you know?" but could not find it in me to ask questions, only to put an arm about her shoulders and lead her, unprotesting, along the passage and into the front room, where she could sit in comfort, while not being in the way.

I saw Marcus and Dr. Cellini go past, and heard Marcus call:

"Did you get him?"

A man called back: "Yes, sir. May I ask what has been happening?"

"I think, officer, if you could hold Mr. Jees for the time being, either Mr. Hunter or I will prefer a charge of attempted assault and an attempt to cause grievous bodily harm. I am — "

"I know who you are," the man said. "Is everything all right in there?"

"As right as it can be for the time being," Dr. Cellini said. "Will you ask your inspector in charge to telephone Chief Superintendent Hardy and say — "

"Mr. Hardy's on his way to Division, sir," replied this man with a penchant for interruption. "Anything we can do inside, sir?"

"No. No one is hurt."

"Very good, sir," the man responded, and almost at once I heard Dr. Cellini's footsteps on the path.

Esmé was sitting in an armchair which rocked slightly to and fro. I saw Marcus, who opened the door for Dr. Cellini, who came in rather slowly, as if he suddenly felt tired. Marcus followed and pushed a chair up for him, and he sat down, with obvious relief, in front of Esmé. As he looked at her, unsmiling, stern, he seemed very old and sad.

What he had said was only now beginning to make sense to me.

Anthony had been killed in mistake for Hilary.

The poisoned chocolates had been meant for her.

George had planned to kill her because he would inherit much of her wealth. Was it true? Could it be true?

Was Dr. Cellini going to try to make Esmé talk, now?

I felt Marcus's hands at my waist, firm, not painful or bruising. He lifted me and I was surprised at the ease with which he did so; the way in which he placed me at one end of the couch and the quietness with which he sat at the other end, and waited. The only noises came from the street; more voices, the slamming of a car door, footsteps; the harsh starting of a car engine, the softer note as it moved away. When it had gone and only silence lingered, Dr. Cellini spoke very quietly, with a gentleness which was almost a caress.

"Mrs. Jees," he said, "you know it can be proved, don't you?"

She did not answer.

"It will be much easier for you if you would make a statement now," Cellini said. "I will help you all I can." When she did not reply, he added with the same gentleness: "If I can tell the police what you tell me they won't be so likely to question you tonight." When her face remained hidden, and her hands, beneath the panoply of her hair, he tried again: "Did you know from the beginning? Or have you only just found out? You don't have to be punished for your husband's crimes, you know. Please let me help you."

She did not answer, and he did not speak again.

I longed to go to the other woman and try to comfort her, but Marcus had a hand on my right arm: restraining me deliberately. So I waited and watched. The barking continued but seemed a long way off; and occasionally became a cry rather than a bark.

At long last, Esmé looked up; and she seemed ten, twenty years older than when I had last seen her; the change was so great that I was shocked. She brushed her hair back from her forehead, and then pressed her hands against her eyes.

She said: "I didn't know — at first.

"He did come to England alone, four years ago, living in London. But he also came before Hilary was in trouble. I — I wondered then why he lied.

"When he kept coming back, I began to think he had a mistress. I thought — I even thought it was you."

And she looked from Dr. Cellini straight across the room at me; and I was astonished; and yet there could be no doubt that she meant what she said: that this was true.

"That was why I — I came over, at least a year ago. His only mistress was Spots here, I soon learned that. I couldn't understand why he preferred to be here, what he was really doing, but then I learned that he became the administrator of the money which Hilary inherited. After a while he told me the truth."

"He told me that once she had been convicted for the murder he could do nothing to help Hilary, except officially advise on, but actually spend, money that was hers; money she would not discover missing until she came out of prison. He — he wasn't sure whether anyone suspected what he had done; whether anyone suspected he had meant to give her poisoned chocolate, so that she should die and Anthony be blamed.

"He — he simply wasn't sure. He didn't feel safe.

"But if he could fake evidence that some other person had killed Anthony, then at least Hilary would not suspect him when she came out of prison. He believed he could explain away the money he had spent by saying it had gone on trying to establish Hilary's innocence. He knew Janetta had been under suspicion and had been ill, and she seemed the obvious one to select."

Esmé stopped; and for the first time since she had started to tell her story, I was aware of the barking of the dog. It seemed very loud again, and she turned and looked towards the door, and said:

"May I have Spots? *Please?*"

"Of course you may," said Cellini gently.

"I'll go with her to let him out," Marcus offered, and left me sitting opposite Dr. Cellini, who smiled at me but did not speak; and again I was impressed by his expression of sadness. But his face brightened when the others returned, the dog's tail beating the air. Spots looked round, obviously for George, but when Esmé told him to sit, he settled promptly by her side and looked up at her, panting.

"So you see, for much of the time I knew," Esmé continued at last. "I did not know all the things he did and planned and said, but I knew the general plan, and supported him."

"Knowing what could happen?" Cellini asked.

"Sure," she said. "Sure. You see — " She broke off.

"Please go on," Cellini said. "There can be so little more."

"You're right," agreed Esmé and for the first time since George had run she actually gave a smile. "I had to go on. We were married. It was his safety, his future which mattered to me." She looked across at me, began to move her hands forward then withdrew them as if she knew she could only be rebuffed. "Janetta," she said, "there was only one thing we hated: that it had to be you. It was a terrible thing to do to someone we liked but whatever else could we do?"

I could only look at her in silence, and was not even sure that I really heard Marcus whisper: "You being you."

"Mrs. Jees," said Dr. Cellini, after a long time when no one spoke, "I think you should let me take you to the police station. An old friend of mine, Chief Superintendent John Hardy will be there and I would like to tell him what you have told me. He will no doubt have to charge you as well as your husband, but he will make everything as easy as he can."

She said chokily: "Thank you."

After a moment when no one moved she looked up in sudden alarm: "But what about Spots? Spots will go mad without us. What about Spots?"

"I think," began Marcus, hesitantly. He gulped, glanced at me, and held a hand out towards the dog. "I think we could be friends and I'm going to need a friend here. May I look after him?"

"Oh, if you would!" cried Esmé.

When she left, she looked quite cheerful; and I am quite sure that it was because she felt certain that Marcus would be kind and gentle towards the dog. Spots actually let himself be taken on a short leash to the kitchen, where there was room at least for him, and then went with me into the street. Dr. Cellini was handing Esmé up into the seat next to the steering wheel of the old car, and two policemen stood watching while a police car followed as a moment later they drove off.

A number of people were at their windows, one or two even at the gates, watching. But no one spoke to us, although a near neighbour said quite clearly:

"I hope that dog isn't going to kick up such a row all night."

For Spots was whining.

We stood at the end of the passage, listening for a while, and I really did not know what to do until Marcus asked in a low-pitched voice:

"Do you need anything else in the kitchen tonight?"

"Not unless you want some tea or coffee," I said.

"If we don't disturb him, he'll soon settle down," Marcus said.

"Will he?" I wondered aloud. "I hope so."

"Let's give it a try," Marcus suggested; and then quite without warning he seized me and lifted me cradled against his chest, and carried me up the stairs as if I were no weight at all. My heart was pounding in a way I had never known it; with a kind of excitement that could have been hysteria but most certainly wasn't fear. Almost before I realised it, I was lying on the small bed, skirt rucked up, breathless;

and he had his right hand, fingers spread wide, over my waist and pinning me down.

He looked down on me.

He asked in a rough voice: "Hate me?"

"I — I ought — I — *no!*"

"*I* hate me," he said.

"Marcus — "

"If you keep on interrupting me I'll walk out of this house and never come back," he growled. He pressed and eased off, pressed and eased off again as he spoke. "I know. I've given you a hell of a time. I know. I've tried to keep you by blackmail and threats. I know. You would have walked out on me long ago if I hadn't lied to you about what you said in your sleep. I *know*. But there are some things *you've* got to know. You can drive a man to desperation. You have driven *me* to desperation. Sometimes I thought you just got sadistic pleasure out of denying me. Sometimes I could have strangled the life out of you. Sometimes I thought that if I did a cave man act and just took you by force it would stir the primeval instincts in you. All it did was make you hate the sight of me. And after that I was just plain man — beast. I know it. I think you drove me to it. I'm bloody sure that if you start that 'I can't bear you to touch me' game again, I'm through. I've nothing to hold you with now except the male in me, my physical strength *and* my handsome face. Either that's got to be enough or it's nothing."

He eased his hand away from me and then said softly: "*Understand?*" and then pressed more firmly than before but with no violence, no savage strength.

I did not answer.

"You've got a choice," he said. "Hate me or love me. Hate me and I'll go, love me and — "

Quite suddenly, his hand was gone; quite suddenly he was on his feet and his back was towards me and quite suddenly I saw his shoulders heave. I was so astounded I could not believe it possible. He was fighting for composure, he might even hate it if I saw that he was crying; or at least if I let him know that I had seen.

I said: "It's strong and firm but it's not big enough for sleeping."

In a muffled voice he asked: "What the hell are you talking about?"

"You mean to say you don't *know*? I thought it was a fixation with you."

"A fixation?" His shoulders stopped heaving and he stood upright, taking his hands from his face. "Oh, blast that bloody dog, it'll keep the neighbours up all night."

"So I have competition for your interest," I said.

He turned to face me. He had been crying but the tears had gone and he looked not fierce but puzzled. His hair was ruffled and he looked quite devastatingly handsome.

"Competition?" he echoed. "I don't understand you. I — oh, good God!"

"Go and bring him upstairs," I suggested, "but make it clear to him that he is not sharing our bed."

Marcus stood looking down on me for a while, not smiling, but with a fierce expression in his eyes. Then he turned and went out and downstairs. He was gone a long time; long enough for me to put on a nightdress, to run a comb loosely through my hair, and to go into the other room. I expected him to lead Spots up when he did come, but he was alone.

"He was hungry," he announced. "You'll have to go and buy some more meat tomorrow."

He stood over me. He had taken his dressing-gown downstairs with him, and wore it now.

Momentarily.

He is quite a magnificent man.

Epilogue

— in the form of a conversation or more truly a
monologue involving Dr. Emmanuel Cellini and
his wife, Felisa, after the trial of George Jees for
the murder of Anthony Grey.

"MANNY, MY DEAR," FELISA CELLINI SAID, "YOU LOOK SO
very tired. Sit down, please, now. I will get you tea and I
have some cheesecake fresh from the oven . . .

"Ah, that is good, you are resting, Manny. Tell me, was
it so very bad? I know, I know, always it is bad when you
give evidence for the prosecution, but — this man, he was
so wicked."

"So wicked?" echoed Cellini. "Wicked, yes. But wholly
evil, no. Unlike his sister who has now the Queen's Pardon,
he has a capacity for badness but also much good lives in
him. I would not have given evidence, you know that, if
John Hardy had not helped me so much, early in the case."

"I know, I know. You torment yourself so much, old
man. Now! This is the very best cheesecake I have made
in years . . ."

"I had to give my opinion of his sanity, which no one
seriously doubted, and of Esmé's."

"She *is* sane, yes?"

"Yes."

"Then should she not be punished?"

"Yes, yes," replied Dr. Cellini, with a rare touch of irritation. "She should be punished as an accessory — a willing accessory. She meets a man and marries him and gives herself completely to him in love, in loyalty, in faithfulness, and because of these things she commits a crime. And in committing the crime she is tainted with evil; by doing what you have done since we were married, Felisa, she does a wicked thing, she tries to help to prove an innocent person guilty. Felisa, my love, this cheesecake is indeed *very* good."

"You like more?"

"Later, please, later." He paused. "Now, more tea will be most welcome . . . Felisa, such a story was told, for once I wish you had been in the public gallery. The sister, this Hilary, was the older by two years and she inherited a very large amount of money, there was some talk of more than a million dollars."

"Such riches to inherit!"

"Such riches to inherit, indeed . . . A fortune within his grasp. And there was a risk that Hilary would spend it not on her husband but on her lover, a possibility George Jees could not contemplate. Yet he could contemplate poisoning the chocolates, about which his sister had told him, and leaving them with her, not knowing it was her custom to give a box to her lover after their evenings together."

Emmanuel Cellini sipped, and his wife looked down at him anxiously, for trials such as this one took so much strength out of him.

She saw a change come over him: a look of benignity; and her eyes lit up because he smiled at her.

"Some good thing happened?" she inquired eagerly.

"Some very pleasing news," agreed Cellini. "And in its way as good as the other is bad. For when I first heard of him it seemed that there was evil, true evil incarnate, in

Marcus Hunter. Instead, it was agony of the spirit and denial of the flesh which warped him. Now — so John Hardy tells me — his wife Janetta is to have a child."

"So soon?" cried Felisa.

"So foolish you can be," reproved Cellini. "There were eight months between the arrests and the trial, and the baby is to be born, John tells me, at the end of next month. She is not lonely now."

"An unborn baby, *lonely*?"

"Oh woman, woman! *Janetta! Janetta* was so lonely and afraid, and now she has a husband whom she loves, and a dog whom she spoils, and soon a child."

"It will be the making of her," Felisa declared roundly.

"The making of her?" echoed Cellini, looking at his childless wife. "If a child is needed to make a woman, my woman, how is it you came to be made?"